Published by Dream House Press
2714 Ophelia Ct
San Jose, CA 95122
Published in San Jose, CA, U.S.A.
E-mail: dreamhousepress@yahoo.com
Phone: (408) 274-4574
Fax: (408) 274-0786

All rights reserved. No part of this publication may be reproduced in any manner without permission in writing, except in the case of brief quotations embodied in critical articles and reviews.

ISBN ten digit: 0-9671555-7-6
ISBN thirteen digit: 978-0-9671555-7-6

Library of Congress Control Number: 2006906450

Printed in the United States of America
Publication date, July 2007

Edited by
Margie Maestas-Flores

Cover Illustration and Production by
Hiram Duran Alvarez
Alvarez Design & Illustration
AlvarezDesign75@yahoo.com

Second Edition Revised

Forgotten Memories

by

Art Rodriguez

Dream House

Dedication

Mother, I remember when I was young and was going through the most difficult times in my life; you were there for me. You were the one who took care of me when I was just a boy. This is why I dedicate this book to you. I am very grateful to have had you in my life for so many years. You will be in my heart forever, and I will be with you forever.

Foreword

When I wrote this book, I wanted to help young people and show them that when difficult problems arise in their families, life continues. It is not the end of the world as most of us feel when we are young and going through negative experiences.

I did not think my mother realized how much my brothers, sister, and I were affected by what happened in *Forgotten Memories*. When I wrote this story, I did not intend to tell her life story to the world. However, I did want to tell my story as a young thirteen-year-old kid, from a thirteen-year-old point of view, through my eyes and my heart.

I wanted my mother to read the manuscript from the beginning to the end, so she could feel the impact of it. In addition, I wanted to show her how this story could help youngsters who are having similar family problems.

Someone in the family told my mother a certain story was in this book. Because of this comment, my mother did not start reading the book the way I wanted her to. She flipped through pages to find the specific part of the manuscript that dealt with her. I received a phone call from a family member informing me that my mother was very upset with me and was going to give me the third degree. I did not want to argue with my mother. She did call that afternoon; however, I was not home. She asked my wife Flora what she thought about my story. Flora told my mother she thought it was written very well and felt it was going to help young people see that they are not the only ones who go through these experiences in life. My mother did not agree with her. She asked Flora to have me return her call when I arrived home. When I received this message, I did not want to call my mother because I knew she was very disturbed. I wanted to give her time to cool off. Three days later, I stopped at her house to visit with her. She said she did not want to stay upset with me; but as long as she was alive, she forbid me to write about her. I tried to explain that I was not writing about her but was telling my story from a kid's point of view.

After hearing her feelings on the matter, I decided to change a few chapters to suit her. I published *Forgotten Memories*.

I am sad to say that my mother passed away on March 11, 2003. I have had much time to reflect on what she expressed. As long as she was alive, I could not write the true story. After much contemplation, I have come to recognize that many young people will benefit from the true story. For that reason, I have adjusted and revised *Forgotten Memories* to tell the real, true story.

I know in my heart that this will benefit adolescents because I went through this difficult experience. It hurt me very much, and I do not wish this same hurt upon anyone else. I want you, young person, to realize that many families are going through serious problems, just as I experienced. Remember, it may be a tough experience in life; but life continues. Things change and time heals. I will never forget it! I know that this event and many other trials, as you have read in my books, made me the person I am today. I know if you persist in your life to do good you can move on when problems surface. Do not let experiences get you so down that you feel as if life is not worth living. Love for others and their love for you will help you get through the rough times in life, and it will heal your heart. What you put into your life, you will get out of your life. So work hard at home, at school, and in whatever you do!

Contents

1 MOM 1

2 A KID'S HEADACHE 11

3 THE GETAWAY 21

4 THE BOXING BOYS 25

5 THE BIG BANDAGE 36

6 THE CHERRY BOMB 42

7 THE DROWNING 55

8 BURNED 65

9 THE TIRE SHOP 73

10 SATURDAY NIGHT 82

11 THAT DREADFUL DAY 91

12 THE HOSPITAL 100

13 THE KNIFE FIGHT 108

14 THE WAIT 117

15 THOSE TERRIBLE WORDS 127

16 THE TURBULENT YEARS 137

17 THE WILD GUYS 146

18 MAKING PEACE 156

Chapter One

Mom

My mother is seventy-one years old. She has been suffering with a bad heart ever since she was in her late forties. As I was driving my car to see her, I thought back to all the pleasant memories of my relationship with her. I stopped my car in front of her house.

A few years ago, Eddie, my brother, bought the house from her. He told her he was going to take care of her for the rest of her life. Eddie had the house remodeled on Virginia Place.

The house from the street appears the same as it did when we were growing up; however, it is completely different on the inside. My mother lives in her portion of the house. She had been very sick the last few weeks because of the damage that was done to her heart from her last heart attack.

I parked the car, turned off the engine, and sat for a few minutes in deep thought. I went back in time and saw my mother sitting on the front grass watching us play. I remembered running into her arms when my brother Eddie was about to rope me. Sitting in the car, I could feel her smile and smell her scent.

I went back to my earliest memories and remembered my mother leaving to the movies with my grandmother. I wanted to go with her so badly. I didn't like my mother to leave me at all, especially with my father who was a very strict man. I was upset because she refused to take me with her. She told me this was her evening with her mother, and I had no choice in the matter. Feeling sad I asked her how long she was going to be gone. She reached for my cheek, squeezed it, then bent down and gave me a big kiss and a hug and said, "Not long, Arthur. Not long. Be good, so your father doesn't get angry with you." I became teary.

I came out of my trance from recalling memories of visiting her. Sitting in the car and thinking of my cherished mother who was very sick, I knew the day was coming when I was going to lose someone who is close and valuable to me. I wiped my eyes, opened the door, and stepped out of the car. I looked around and again remembered many events that took place in my childhood. "Ay, ay, ay, Mom. When that day comes, I am really going to miss you," I thought.

As I approached the front door, I thought of the conversation I had with my sister Mildred or, as we called her, Tita. She told me my mother was very sick the night before; Mildred had to drive her to the hospital.

The front door was locked. I walked around the side of the house. This was where we as children had to go because my father had a rule: kids could not use the front door. Actually, at the present time the front door was the entrance to my brother Eddie and his wife Martha's portion of the house. The side door now belonged to my mother. The walkway around the side was very pretty with green foliage that my mother planted and maintained.

I never thought when I was a child that I would see my mother become old and sick. I felt and believed the time would never come. I imagined she would be here forever and felt she would always be with me. I would never lose her.

When I was going through the difficult times in my life, even though I didn't want to burden my mother with my problems, I would go to her house and lay on her bed next to her. She knew something was wrong; however, she would never ask. She knew I just needed her comfort.

As a man I always felt like a child when I was with her, a child in her arms.

I opened the door and saw my mother sitting on the sofa watching TV. "Hi, Mijo!" (Mijo, an expression of endearment.) "I'm glad you came over. I was just thinking about you." My mother appeared droopy and not well at all. She had dark circles around her eyes.

"How are you, Mom?" I asked as I bent over and gave her a kiss and then a big hug, not wanting to let go of her.

"Oh, I don't feel good. My doctor called, and I told him I stopped the medicine he gave me. I told him I couldn't take it anymore. It was getting worse. I felt a lot sicker after I started it."

"And what did he say?"

"He said it was OK. He said I should go in so we can talk and see what else he can do for me. Ay, Mijo, I feel so weak. It's because my heart is not working right. I just can't do anything. I want to go outside and work on my plants, but I can't," she said sadly.

"Well, Mom, maybe in a few days you'll be feeling better, good enough to go outside and do a little gardening. Maybe the new medicine the doctor is going to give you will get you going again," I replied, knowing my mother was a very sick woman and that this may never happen.

"And I don't know why my legs hurt so much. They feel like I sprained them. Yesterday when you came over, they felt bad; but now they're worse. I wish I were well and could run like when I was young."

"I know, Mom. I know you do," I replied, not really knowing what to say.

Despite her ill health, there was one good thing, my mother's new religious beliefs. She now belonged to a religion that teaches she will live again on this earth and be in good health. It helped her get by every day.

I stayed and chatted with my mother a little more, letting her tell me about all the pains and disappointments she had. I didn't mind listening to her as I thought back and remembered all the times when I was a little guy. I would run to my mother and complain to her. She would sit me on her lap and listen. She never turned me away. Today I sat with her and listened. I wished I could fix all that was wrong with her health. Soon I had to leave.

"Well, Mom, I have to go. I have a lot of things to take care of, but I had to come and see you for a bit," I said as I stood.

"Ay, Mijo, thank you for coming. You are so good, and I love you so much." Hearing those few words, I fought back my tears.

I walked to my mother's side, bent down, and held her tightly. Usually I gave her a kiss and a nice hug; however, on this day I wanted to hold my mother longer. I hugged her tight and wouldn't release her. She felt the hug and sensed how I felt.

She whispered in my ear as I was holding her, "I love you, Arturito."

"I love you too, Mom."

That night I lay in my bed and knew I wasn't going to sleep very well, thinking of those forgotten memories. I saw my mother when she was young and all the problems she was having with my father and with life. I thought back to when my buddy Phillip came over with good news on a particular day.

I was sound asleep when I heard a voice call out in a whisper, "Arthur! Arthur, wake up!" Then I heard a tap on the window.
Waking up, I thought, "Who in the heck is calling me so early in the morning?" I could see the sun had just risen. It was going to be a warm summer morning in San Jose, California.
During this time my mother and father had been having a lot of trouble in their marriage. On the weekends my father had been staying out with his friends. My poor mother was left alone too long without her husband. She didn't like his staying out with friends at the bar, not knowing where else he would go; however, she had little to say about it. He did what he wanted, and that was it. On the other hand my mother had grown tired of waiting up for my father; she no longer waited. In fact, in the past year she had been going out without my father knowing about it.
Mom had befriended the Lopez girls' mother who lived down the street. Sarah, the Lopez's mother came from a large family. Sarah's sisters were also now close to Mom. My father thought she was spending time at Sarah's home when, in fact, she was hanging out with their group of friends and going out to the clubs alot.
"Arthur! Arthur, are you there?" shouted Phillip.
I stepped out of bed and walked to the window, a window that was high for me to reach. Under it was a nightstand that I could stand on to look out or to climb out if I had to do so. In no way did I want my friend to wake up my father. Dad would be very upset with me if he knew I had a friend over so early on a Sunday morning.
As I was opening the window, I saw Phillip standing outside, waiting in anticipation with the good news he had brought me. He was smiling like a cat who caught a mouse. Phillip was holding two large Coke bottles, but the bottles didn't contain Coke. The liquid in the bottles was a yellowish color.

I pushed the window up; it was tight and made a noise. I looked behind me, hoping I didn't wake up anyone. Looking back at Phillip and raising my finger to my lips, I indicated for him to be very quiet. Phillip knew the way my father was and didn't want to make any trouble, even though that was why he came. Trouble to us was fun.

"Hey, Arthur, my mother and Manuel had a party last night and left all this beer," he said with a big smile. Phillip had one of those large jaws that made his smile really big. Phillip continued, "They have a big keg of beer and left about a fourth of it. They're still sleeping!" he said happily, holding up two Coke bottles, ready to have a good time and wanting me to join him.

"Really? Cool, man!" I said excitedly. During this time my friends and I would try to find ways to buy beer on the weekends, even though we were only fourteen years old.

"Come on, man! Let's go! What are you waiting for? Manuel and my mother are going to get up pretty soon. I already got two bottles, but we need to get more bottles if it's going to last all day!"

Manuel was Phillip's stepfather. He was a good man and really tried to work with Phillip and his brother Jerry. Jerry accepted the goodness and love Manuel was trying to give him; however, Phillip never wanted to befriend his stepfather. He felt no one could love him as his real father had. Phillip wanted his real father to come home and live with them again; he would do anything if he could only have that relationship back.

"OK, wait. I'll be right back. I have to get dressed. Just wait. I'll try not to take long," I said as I closed the window, turned around to get my clothes, and started to dress. It was going to be a fun day with all that beer. "Phillip and I are going to party!" I thought.

"Arthur, where you going? Who's that outside?" my older brother Eddie asked.

Eddie was two years older than I. On the weekends I would fix my bed with my pillows to make it seem as if I were asleep. Then I would crawl out the window and go out. When I returned, I would crawl back into the window and go to bed. This was a very dangerous thing. If my father had ever caught me, it would mean really big trouble for me, maybe even death!

"I'm going with Phillip, Eddie. I'll be back later. I should be back before everybody's up," I replied, knowing that was probably not true.

Eddie sat up on the top bunk as he said, still waking up, "Man, Arthur, if Dad finds out you're gone, he is going to be really mad! Did he come home last night? You better check before you go. Because if he's here and he sees you left without asking, you're going to be in big trouble!"

As I was buckling my pants, I thought about what my brother said. I knew Eddie was right. He always made sense when it came to things like this. "Yeah, your right. I'll go check."

"Good. Be careful. Don't wake him up, or you aren't going anywhere!" Eddie exclaimed as he lay back down on his bed.

If my father were to hear me, he would yell out, "WHO IS UP? ARTURO, IS THAT YOU?" I never understood how he always knew it was me. If he were to yell out for me, I had better answer and fast! If he did call, he would want to know what I was doing up so early. He would then send me back to bed and tell me I was not to get up until the house was alive with activity. When my father said something, I would always comply, knowing he meant business.

During this time my father and I were not getting along. When I was younger, I would always be beaten with the belt on a regular basis. Now that he was going out a lot and I was getting older, he wouldn't hit me with the belt.

I stepped into the kitchen as quietly as possible. I thought I heard someone, but I wasn't sure. Everything was quiet. If Dad was home and I made the slightest noise, I would wake him. It would then be as Eddie had said; I wouldn't be going anywhere. If he wasn't home, I would be able to do whatever I wanted. My mother was so nice; she would say OK to anything I would ask, not knowing I was really up to no good.

Our father was the kind of man who required us, Eddie and me, to finish at least one hour of work in the yard when we arrived home from school, believing it would make us responsible workers when we became older. We didn't like it very much because all of our friends on Virginia Place played in the street as soon as they arrived home from school, but we had to pull weeds. On Saturday we were required to start our work in the yard from sunup until sundown. During this time my father was becoming lax. He was going out all the time and this was creating problems with my mother.

Once I was sure no one was up, I stepped into the living room very slowly. I didn't want to give my father a reason to tell me I couldn't leave. If I went with Phillip after my father told me I couldn't, I knew what the consequences would be. If he didn't tell me anything and I went, it wouldn't be as bad.

In the living room we had a big window facing the street. It had light green drapes that hung down to the floor. The drapes were closed. I had to put my knees on the sofa in order to see if my father's Cadillac was in the driveway. As my knee pressed on the sofa, the sofa squeaked. It wasn't loud; however, because the house was so quiet, I felt as if it could be heard in every room.

I froze, hoping my father didn't hear the noise. I hoped he had drank a lot the night before. If he had, it would be difficult to wake him. Even though my father stayed out all night, at times he would still get out of bed early, turn on his music, and spend the day in the living room, reading and watching TV.

I didn't hear anything, feeling glad I didn't wake him. I pulled the drapes back and hoped his car was gone. If it was, I no longer had to be so careful. I wished! I wished! It was there! I was very disappointed.

What was I going to do? If I left the house without asking permission, I knew I was in for it when I returned. My father would have a fit knowing I left without asking.

Because my mother and father were having so much trouble in their marriage, my mother had been sleeping in my sister Tita's bedroom. In years past my mother was always submissive to my father. She was now tiring of his going out and staying out all night, sometimes leaving on Friday after work and not coming home until Sunday. In this case he only returned on Sunday because he had to go to work the following day.

My father had been planning on returning to Mexico. He had been saying that as soon as American Can Company closed down he was leaving. I never understood if he was planning on taking all of us with him or if he was planning on leaving us and going alone.

I thought it would be better if I asked my mother's permission to go with Phillip. In order to do that, however, I had to get to her room and pass in front of my father's bedroom.

I hoped the door was closed, as it was most of the time. If my father was awake, he would see me and ask what I was doing. If I told him I was going to speak to my mother, he would tell me to go to my bedroom because I was going to wake up everybody in the house.

As I approached his room, I saw that his bedroom door was open. My stomach felt as if it had butterflies. It was a feeling of great nervousness. I didn't want to step in front of the bedroom door and take a chance. I knew if my father saw me, my plans of having a cool Sunday would be impossible. Maybe I should just leave and take my chances on the consequences when I returned. I thought, "Maybe if I go with Phillip, I can return in a little while, as soon as we fill more bottles and save them for later. Then I can ask my mother when she is up and around."

I had an idea! I could get to my mother's bedroom if I crawled on my stomach. My father wouldn't be able to see me, and it would save me from his yelling and name calling if I had her permission.

I lowered my body to the floor and started to move across the hall into Tita and Mom's bedroom. As I reached the front of my father's doorway, I heard him make a sound with his throat, indicating to me that he wasn't asleep. I didn't move for a second. I looked over and saw him under the covers, holding his arms up as if he were looking at something. If he were to hear me and sit up, I would be done for it. He would give me the third degree and try to find out what I was doing.

Once I knew he didn't see me, I continued moving slowly across the hallway. My mother's door was shut, but not all the way. There was a two-inch opening. I reached forward and pushed the door open very slowly, hoping it didn't squeak and get my father's attention. I dragged myself a little more, reaching the bedroom where my mother was sleeping.

My mother slept with my sister in her twin-size bed. I bent down on one knee next to her bed and whispered, "Mom. Mom." I didn't want to call too loudly and let my father hear me. The second time I called a little louder and shook her a bit.

My mother opened her eyes and saw me looking down over her. "What, Mijo? What happened?"

I whispered, "Nothing happened, Mom. I want to ask you if it's all right if I go with my friend Phillip. I'll be back in awhile."

"Where are you going, Mijo?" my mother asked as she was waking up. My mother was speaking very low. She also didn't want to wake my father.

"I want to go to his house, and then we're going to the flea market for awhile."

The flea market was a market where people went to sell their things; some called it a swap meet. Stands were set up, and both new and used items were sold. We had a friend whose father had a tire shop at the flea market.

"OK, Arthur, but be careful," my mother said softly as she reached up and stroked my hair. She ran her hand down my cheek.

I bent down and gave my mother a kiss and a hug. "Bye, Mom. Thank you."

"Bye, Mijo. Be careful," she repeated as she smiled and moved her hand across my hair again. Mother appeared very sad. She had an expression I had never before observed. Something wasn't right. I wanted to lie down with her and have her hold me in her arms. Bending over, I gave my mother another kiss. She reached up and pulled me down to her, squeezing me tightly for a few seconds.

"I love you, Arthur. Always remember that. I love you so much," she whispered as she held me tighter.

"I love you too, Mom. Mom, what's wrong?"

"Nothing, Mijo. I just love you and wanted to tell you."

As she held me, I felt her face wet with tears. "Are you sure you're all right, Mom?"

"I'm OK, Arthur. Be careful. All right?" she asked as she let go of me. I stood up and sat on her bed next to her, holding her hand. I didn't say anything and neither did she. Wishing to stay and knowing something was definitely wrong with Mom, I knew she was either sick or sad. Whatever it was, I hurt for her. I had grown really close to Mom now that I was a teenager.

"Mom?" I asked.

"Yes, Arturito."

"What is it? What's wrong? Is there anything I can do?"

"No, Arthur. It's all right. You go with your friend Phillip; and be good, OK?" Mom said as she tried not to cry. She now spoke in a more composed manner, not wanting to alarm me.

"I will, Mom," I answered as I pulled away. I wanted to stay and lie next to her for a little while, but I thought of Phillip waiting outside for me. Still holding her hand, I said, "Bye, Mom."

"Bye, Mijo. See you later."

I turned and stepped to the doorway. Again I lowered my body to the floor and crawled, this time a little quicker, knowing my father didn't see me the first time. I heard my father make another noise and knew it was just a matter of time before he would get up and leave his room. I had to leave fast. Once I was across the hallway, I stood and made my way back to my bedroom.

Back in my bedroom I closed the door very slowly. "Arthur, is Dad home?" Eddie asked, hoping I had come to my senses if he were home.

"Yeah, he is," I answered as I opened the window.

"What are you doing? Are you still going even though he's here? Are you crazy? Man, Arthur, you're really going to get it if you take off."

When I had the window open, I stuck my head out and looked for Phillip. He was sitting against the house and waiting.

"Hey, Phillip, I'll be right out. Let me put on my shoes."

"OK, don't take too long. Manuel might get up, and then we won't be able to get the beer."

"OK, I won't," I answered as I turned and sat on the bottom bunk.

"You're crazy, Arthur," Eddie said as he leaned over the bunk. "When Dad gets up and you're not here, he's going to be really mad!"

"I don't care. I asked Mom, and she said it was OK."

Eddie didn't say anything for a few seconds. He probably was thinking of all the problems our parents were having.

I also was having a very difficult time with my father. I even ran away not long before this.

Chapter Two

A Kid's Headache

Every morning my mother rose early to make my father's breakfast before he left for work. She would also prepare burritos for his lunch. My father was always irritated with my mother for one reason or another. When he became upset with her, he wouldn't leave a subject alone but continued to nag her.

I was seven years old at this time. My mother wouldn't say much, knowing it would make things worse. She started cooking while my father took his shower. The shower was in the back part of the house, down the hallway. Our bedroom was next to the bathroom. As soon as my father was finished with his shower, he would go into the kitchen and continue his nagging where he left off. Speaking in Spanish he harped, "Millie, I told you what I wanted; and you did not do it! I told you to do it right, and see what you did? Ay, Millie!"

My mother wouldn't respond. She knew if she did, it would make things worse. She listened and continued her cooking. I held my blankets over my head, hoping it would stop. He continued speaking roughly, "Millie, did I not tell you? Answer me! I said answer me! Now look what happened! You really messed things up! Millie! Millie! Millie!" On and on he went.

My mother was tired of it. Nonetheless, she was scared to reply. "Joe, I forgot. I'm sorry."

"You forgot? What do you mean you forgot? How do you forget something like that?" My father raised his voice even more because my mother said something to defend herself.

She served him his food as he sat in his customary place. "Ay, Millie! ¿Qué pasa (what's happening)? Look at my frijoles (beans)!

They are dry! How do you expect me to eat this? Ay, mujer (woman), what is wrong with you, ¡estupida!"

With the dry frijoles he had something else to be angry about before he left for work. On and on it went through his whole meal. I held my hands over my ears, not wanting to hear it anymore. Now he was upset over his food not being cooked to his liking. My mother was a good cook, but trying to cook for her husband under these conditions was very trying. I hated every second of it. Every morning it was the same. Once in a while my father would wake up in a good mood, but this didn't happen very often.

It was still dark outside. My father went out the front door. I was relieved he was gone and stayed in my bed, hoping he would go to the bar after work and not come home until late. The house was quiet. My mother went into the bathroom.

I heard the front door open. "Oh, no!" I thought, "He's back!"

"Millie!" he yelled. "Millie! ¿Donde esta (Where are you?) Millie?"

My mother raced out of the bathroom and answered, "What, Joe? What is it now?" She knew my father found or thought of another reason to be upset.

"¡Tu hijo (Your son), Arturo! ¡Estupido! ¡Huevon (Egghead)! He left the water on all night!" my father yelled, adding some obscene words. I knew he was really angry. As he stomped toward my bedroom door, he was swearing in Spanish.

I recalled the evening before my father had called me from my bedroom, telling me to go turn the water off on the front lawn. I was on the way to the front yard when a friend came around the side of the house to visit. I met him, and we talked for a while. Then I went back into the house and forgot about turning off the water.

"Oh, no!" I sat up in my bed, terrified. "What did I do? What should I say to stop this?" I felt my life was going to end in just a few seconds. I wanted to cry right there, but I thought maybe there was something else I could do to save myself.

"Joe, don't wake him up! He's asleep!" my mom exclaimed, following closely as he headed toward my bedroom. She knew my father usually didn't like waking us. For some reason he always had a compassionate feeling for us when we were sleeping.

I lay back down on my bed and closed my eyes just as my father opened the door, making sure not to move. I knew if I did move, I was going to receive a beating right that second.

My father stood at the door for what seemed to be a long time. He called in a low voice, "Arturo!" I knew he wanted me to be awake. "Arturo!" he called again. Then a third time, "Arturo!" I knew I should answer, but I didn't want to respond.

Not moving a muscle, I hoped he wouldn't try to wake me. I didn't know who God was, but I sure prayed to Him as I lay there at that moment. I begged Him to get my father to go to work and to leave me alone. Maybe by the time he came home, he would be cooled down and be more understanding.

"¡Este muchacho estupido (This stupid boy)!" He closed my door. I took a deep breath! I was sure relieved.

"Ha, ha, ha, ha," he sung his sarcastic laugh as he walked back down the hallway toward the front of the house. "Tell Arturo that when I get home I am going to get him good! Do you know how much money he wasted? Do you?" He continued his questions in Spanish as if it were my mother's fault.

My stomach turned. I was really feeling sick. My mother didn't reply; she knew better. My father said a few more words; then I heard the front door open and close. I stayed under my covers, feeling glad he had to go to work. At the same time I worried about what was going to take place when he arrived in the evening.

I stayed in my bed worrying for an hour. My mother opened the bedroom door and said, "Time to get up, boys." I stretched, acting as if I had been asleep all morning.

"Arturito, did you hear your father this morning?"

"No, what did he say," I answered, wanting my mother to tell me anything I didn't hear.

"He was upset at you for leaving the water on all night. Ay, Arthur, you shouldn't have left it on. Did you forget?"

I pretended to be surprised and said, "Oh, no! I did? What did Dad say?"

"He said he's going to deal with you when he gets home this evening."

I was really scared, even though I heard most of what he said earlier. I positively knew what it meant when my father said he was going to deal with me when he got home. It didn't mean sitting down and having a nice talk.

I dressed for school but was too nervous to eat anything for breakfast. When I stepped out the front door, I saw how the water flooded the front yard as well as the back. Ten million gallons must have been wasted, enough to water the field behind our house. Now I knew why my father was going to deal with me when he got home!

All day at Mayfair Elementary School, I worried about how hard and how long I was going to be beaten. I wondered if I were going to live through the evening, not thinking I was and trying to develop a plan. I couldn't come up with one. I had to think of something before my dad returned from work because I didn't want to get hit. There wasn't anything to stop him. When he hit, he hit!

At 2 p.m. as I was nearing my home from school, a light went on in my head. I knew what I was going to do! My plan was to wear a few pairs of pants and a few shirts when I received my beating. This way it wouldn't hurt.

There was about an hour-and-a-half before my father arrived home from work. I was really nervous because I knew what my dad was going to do when he got home.

The thought of running away occurred to me, but where would I run? I wanted to call someone for help, but no one would listen to a kid who said his father was going to kill him. If I said my father was going to beat me uncontrollably, they would say, "Good, you probably need it." In those days it was no big deal.

I hurried into the house. My mother had started dinner. My father always wanted his dinner when he arrived home from work.

"Hi, Mom."

"Hi, Arthur. Are you ready for your father?"

I didn't know why my mother asked me such a question. I was never ready for him.

"Has he called today?" I asked worriedly. Generally he called everyday.

"Yes, he did."

"What did he say?" I stood still and hoped he had forgotten about the water.

"He wanted to know if I told you he was upset with you. He also wanted to know your explanation for leaving the water on all night."

"What did you tell him, Mom?" I hoped my mother said something in my defense.

"I told him you did not have one, or you did not give it to me. Your father did not like that very much and said he was going to deal with you when he got home."

Now I felt as if my mother really blew it for me! I felt she could have said something to help me.

I didn't know if my plan was going to work. I did have to do something and didn't want to be whipped, that was for sure!

"Well, Arthur? Why didn't you turn it off? I heard your father tell you to go and turn the water off."

"I forgot, Mom. That's it. I just forgot. I saw Donald outside, and I started talking to him, and I forgot."

"You better think of a better reason if you don't want to get spanked! Forgetting is not going to do it with your father. You know him!"

My mother was right. I did know him, but it was the truth!

Mom said my father informed her to tell me not to go anywhere. He wanted me to be home when he arrived. At that moment I thought of my plan! I was scared but hoped what I was planning was going to work.

I walked into my bedroom and opened my dresser drawer, taking out and putting on five pairs of pants and five t-shirts. I also took out three pairs of socks. At this point I started to feel safe. However, it didn't seem as if it was going to be enough. I put on two more t-shirts.

I was ready an hour before my father arrived home. Once in a while my father would arrive home a few minutes early. This was very unlikely; however, I didn't want to take any chances with my life. I left my bedroom and walked to the kitchen, hoping my mother wouldn't notice all the clothes I was wearing. I knew my mother had started cooking because I could smell the carnitas and tortillas all over the house. When my mother cooked, one could be out on the street and could almost taste the food.

Right away my mother noticed I looked fat. "Arthur, why . . ." She stood in front of the stove, stopped what she was doing, and stared at me. She started to laugh, knowing what I had planned.

"Do you think it will work, Arthur? I don't know; your father is pretty smart, Mijo."

"Aw, he won't know. And it won't hurt either. If this works, I'll wear a lot of stuff all the time!"

"But you know, Arthur, if your father notices what you are doing, he is going to be more upset with you. You know what that will mean. You will get it a lot worse. He'll probably make you take everything off and spank you without any clothes."

I thought of what Mom said. She was right. I thought of Dad spanking me as I rolled on the floor, bare skinned. What should I do? I decided to take my chances.

"He won't notice. I know he won't," I said confidently. Then I thought, "If he's able to tell, he might make me take off all my clothes and then whip me with nothing on!"

"OK, Arthur, we'll see."

With that comment I knew my mother wasn't going to tell my father anything. What a relief!

"I think I'll go in the front and pull weeds until he gets home. Maybe if he sees me, he won't spank me as much," I told my mother as I started to walk away. Mom shook her head, not believing I was going to try to fool my father by wearing layers of clothes.

I went out to the front and waited for his car, hoping he stayed with his friends drinking beer and forgetting about me. Wishful thinking!

Our house was on a dead-end street. The other houses on the street were a little older than ours. The house directly across the street from ours used to have an old barn standing beside it. This was when there were no other houses on our street.

The street in front of our home had giant potholes due to the mud puddles that formed during the winter when the road was a mess. Fields surrounded our street. The field behind our house belonged to the Prusch family. It was a dairy farm with long, green grass that the family kept watered for the cows. At times the cows would come up to the barbed-wire fence behind our house, and we would give them grass to eat. A few times we even tried to mount the cows to ride them. No such luck, they would never allow it. The field at the end of Virginia Place had nothing but long grass on it. The same was true also of the field behind the homes across the street from us.

I pulled weeds as fast as I could. It was a mess, and I became muddy quickly because of all the water from the previous night.

Once I had a good pile, I walked across the street to talk to my friend Jerry. We sat on his front grass and kept an eye out for my father's car.

Jerry and I were in the same class later at Lee Mathson Junior High School. He was all right, except that he was teased because he had a feminine way about him. I thought he was OK since I knew him for so long. Jerry felt sorry for me, knowing what had happened with the water. He also knew how tough my father could be, seeing it firsthand as a result of living across the street.

As Jerry and I were speaking, I saw my father's beige car turning the corner two blocks away by the Pink Elephant. The Pink Elephant Market was a shopping center owned by the Murphy family.

I ran across the street to my pile of weeds and hoped my father had not noticed me crossing the road. He told my mother to tell me not to leave the yard. I would receive a harder beating if he saw that I had left. Once I reached our yard, I squatted down by the plants in front of our living room window and started to pull weeds.

My father drove up; right away he noticed me. As he stepped out of his car, I called out, "Hi, Dad!"

My father looked at me and extended his hand, calling out. "Arthur, in the house! Right now!" At least he didn't notice how fat I looked.

I knew what was going to happen. I wanted to tell him, "Look, Dad, I'm pulling weeds! You like us to work. Look. I'm working!"

I stood. He was already walking toward the front door with me right behind him. He waited for me to enter first. I was hoping he didn't notice, as my mother had, that I was wearing five pairs of pants and six t-shirts and that I looked like a blimp.

As soon as we entered the house, I turned around and faced my father. He was already taking off his belt.

"Arthur, I told you last night to turn the water off! Do you know how much money you cost me?"

My father was always worried about money. He went shopping at places where he could save money, even buying clothes at cheap places; however, he never bought used clothes. It was against his ways. Dad and Mom would go to a warehouse and buy our cereals at a discount price. My father could then enjoy the better things of life and give himself more money to spend when he went out with his friends. The food he bought was good; we didn't mind. Every week he would also send money to Mexico to help his mother and family there.

We didn't like the clothes he bought us one bit. Sometimes my friends would laugh at me because of the strange shoes Dad bought me.

Even though I was wearing all those extra clothes, I still hated what was happening. I didn't want it to happen. I hated it!

"Dad, can I say something? Dad?"

"I told you to turn off the water ¡pendejo (fool)!"

"But, Dad! Let me explain. Please, Dad!"

"Explain what? ¡Estupido! You wasted water, and water is money! There is nothing to explain!"

"But, Dad! Please, Dad! Please! I won't do it again! I won't! I promise!"

The first swing of the belt came toward me, and I braced myself for the pain. The belt wrapped around my back. It didn't hurt at all; however, I didn't want to give my father any indication that I was wearing alot of extra clothes.

The force of the belt had knocked me to the floor. I wanted to make this look really good. I yelled, "Dad, please stop! Stop!"

"¡Cobarde (coward)! Stand up! I said, stand up!"

He swung the belt three more times, trying to make me get to my feet. I tried to stand but had a difficult time since my father wasn't letting up on the beating. I thought if I didn't cry, even though it didn't hurt, he would never stop. So I cried as I always did, partly because it terrified me when my father was so angry. I remember feeling as if it were the end of the world, and nothing could stop it. I rolled on the floor, trying to get farther away from him as he was swinging the belt uncontrollably and following me as I rolled.

The unthinkable then occurred! The belt buckle hit me in the head. I yelled with a cry of panic. Now I wasn't trying to fake my crying. I was really crying! It appeared as if my father was now getting some satisfaction.

I rolled on the floor and made my way to the hallway. I had my hands in front of me as the belt buckle approached me. I yelled, "Stop, Dad! Please Stop!"

My father yelled back, "¡Cobarde! Stand up! Put your hands

down! Take it like a man!"

I again rolled on the floor, raising my legs to hold back the blows. The belt was hitting my bear arms, and it really hurt. As I was doing this, I was scooting down the hallway, screaming and yelling, pleading at the same time. "Stop, Dad, please! I won't do it again, Dad! Please! Please! I promise!"

Another blow hit my head with the buckle. I didn't think I could live through this much longer. My short life appeared before me! I knew I was going to die soon, and the end of the world was surely going to occur now.

My father stopped. He looked tired from the aggressive, exhausting beating. He yelled, "Go to your room!" Even though he yelled and told me to go to the bedroom, he was still swinging the belt. "Don't come out until I tell you to."

I stood up and ran, trying to avoid any swings from my father's belt as I left. Two more swings struck my back before I was out of range. I went to my bedroom, closed the door, and hoped my father didn't call me back. Waiting a little while to make sure it was over, I removed all the extra clothes. I laid on my bed still sobbing a bit. My head had two big welts from the belt buckle.

In a little while I could hear my father and mother talking and laughing in the kitchen. I didn't know why they were laughing. I lay still, trying to make out what was being said.

It was impossible to understand how they could be laughing after almost killing their own son. I stepped to the door and opened it a little in order to hear. I still couldn't make out what they were saying. "How could a bad mood turn into a good mood so fast?" I wondered.

In a little while Eddie came into the room and told me, "Dad said you can come out now. He's outside."

I wondered how he moved outside so fast when he was talking to my mother just a second earlier. If he was outside and he didn't call me, I didn't want to go outside with him. I stepped into the kitchen where my mother was setting the table. She looked at me as I entered and asked, "Well, did it hurt?"

I sat on a chair and answered bravely, "What? Did what hurt? The spanking? Na, it was like this," I answered as I brought up my index finger to my tongue, licked it, then wiped it on my pants. I continued, "It felt like that! It didn't hurt at all."

My mother smiled, knowing I was trying to be funny. "Ay, ay, ay, Arthur! Then why did you cry so much?"

Just as I was going to answer, my father walked into the house through the back door. I didn't say anything, not wanting my father to know what I did. If he knew, he might want to hit me again. I thought, "Oh no, I wish I was still in my bedroom."

"¿Qué pasa (What's up)?" Dad asked as he stood at the entrance of the kitchen.

"He said it didn't hurt," Mom replied and then laughed.

My father laughed with her and added, "It did not hurt? I think it did from the way he was llorando (crying). Maybe I better spank him again!"

I thought I was in for it, but my father laughed as if the whole thing was a joke.

Chapter Three

The Getaway

I rolled out the window as Eddie was still trying to talk me out of joining Phillip.

Once outside, I said, "Let's get out of here before my dad gets out of bed."

We walked around the side of the house. Before proceeding to the front, I told Phillip, "Hey, what if my father is looking out the window? I think you should go first and see if he is. If he's not, then I'll come out."

"What if he is? What if he tells me something or asks me what I'm doing? What should I say?"

"Just tell him you aren't doing nothing. What can he say? You're not his son. You can do whatever you want."

Phillip didn't like this very much because he had respect for my father, and he really didn't want to lie to him. "If I see him, I'll go and talk to him and ask if you can come out. That way I don't have to lie to him."

"No, that's not a good idea. Then I won't be able to go. Let's jump the back fence and go through the trailer court. It'll be safer. I don't want to get caught." A few years ago a trailer court had been built behind our house.

Phillip went over the ten-foot fence first. I followed him. Our back yard was cut in two sections. The back half was dirt, and the front half was lawn we planted. It was a big yard.

Just as I went over, I thought I saw someone at the back screen door. I felt my stomach turn with a worried feeling, thinking it was my father. Phillip said, "Oh no! Was that your dad?"

"Did you see him too? I thought I was seeing things. Quick, let's get out of here! Run!"

We both took off. I didn't look back to see if it was my father for sure. Phillip was running in front of me.

The trailer court was quiet. Everyone slept in on Sunday mornings.

Phillip started to tell me something. I interrupted him and said, "Shh, these people are sleeping. We don't want to wake them up."

I didn't think my father would try to follow me; he wasn't that kind of man. He would wait for me to arrive home and then take care of what needed to be handled.

Just two months before this, I became angry with my father and ran away. Each day I was away, I called my mother and let her know where I was and how I was doing. I didn't want her to worry about me. After four days my father told my mother to tell me I could return home.

"Hey, man, you think it was really your father? Man, if it was, maybe we better hide!"

"I don't think so. He was in his room when I left. And if he did get up, he would go into the bathroom first, like he always does."

I was now walking fast. Trying to talk and run was difficult. We came out of the trailer court and crossed the street into the field behind Phillip's house. I continued, "And if it was him, I know my father. He would never come out here to chase after me. He'll just wait until I get home later."

"What do you think he'll say when he tells you something later?" Phillip asked.

"I'll just tell him my mom said I could come."

"Yeah, but what if he asks your mom, then what?"

"No problem. I asked my mom, and she said I could go to your house and then to the flea market."

"Yeah? Then why in the heck are we hiding from him?"

"Man, Phillip, you ask too many questions!"

Our street had only two blocks. Phillip lived one block down on Virginia Place, closer to King Road. He lived next door to the Lopez girls' house. During my early years I played with the kids on our block; during my teenage years I hung around with people from farther down the street and from other neighborhoods. I also hung out with my brother Eddie's friends.

The day I was told Phillip moved in, I wondered what kind of kid he was. I thought maybe he was a sissy or was one of those brainy guys. It turned out he was just like me, always willing to take chances because taking chances was fun. Phillip seldom said no when asked to do things. Phillip was OK.

When we arrived at his house, he went in to make sure his stepfather Manuel and his mother were still sleeping. In a few minutes he came out with three more empty Coke bottles and a big bag. Happily he said, "I found these, but we need more. I wonder where we can get more bottles."

I thought for a minute. He had two bottles already. Both were full when he reached my house. Now one was half-empty; we both had taken some drinks out of it. This made five party packs of Coke bottles.

"Hey, man, I think you have enough. Unless we're going to stay out for a few days! Hey, don't forget I have to go home later. And besides, I know I'll get really high with maybe one-and-a-half of those. That's plenty, Phillip!"

Phillip thought for a moment. He replied, "Let's go into the garage and fill 'em up. Maybe it'll be enough."

Manuel and Elodia had their party in the garage. There were colored balloons still hanging from the ceiling and bright ribbons from wall-to-wall. Everything looked a mess.

"What kind of party did they have, Phillip? A wild one?"

He laughed and answered, "Yeah, a wild one all right. My cousin and me drank some last night, and everyone was so drunk they didn't even notice we were getting beer. It was my mother's birthday."

Why didn't you invite me, man? I would've come if there was free beer!"

He laughed again and said, "I know you would have. I don't know, man. I didn't think about it. I will next time."

Phillip started to fill a bottle. I had to pump the keg to get the pressure up so the beer would release. As the bottle was filling, Phillip said, "I think you're right. This should be enough. I'm already feeling high. I don't know if I can drink a lot more. Maybe we better not take all five bottles. What do you think?"

"I think we should. What if Tómas at the flea market wants some? It won't be good if we're going to his shop to get high and we don't even take him some. I think he won't like it very much. What do you think?"

Phillip laughed again and said, "He'll think we are dirty guys, man! Yeah, I think you're right, Arthur."

I shook the keg of beer to see how much it had left. It still had a lot of beer. When we filled our bottles, the keg felt the same. This was good because Manuel and Elodia would never know we took their beer.

Phillip was a short guy. He had broad shoulders and short, curly, black hair. He had a big jaw that made his smile stretch all the way across his face. Phillip was the type of guy that no matter what we were doing, even being chased by the cops, he thought it was fun.

As we were walking out the back door of the garage, I thought of all the different times we had done things in Phillip's yard. Just a few weeks before we found Manuel's shotgun. We shot it off in the backyard. We then had to hide it along with all the cartridges. When the cops arrived, we would say we didn't hear or do anything. In a little while they would receive another report about another shotgun blast at the same address. Man, we had a lot of fun in Phillip's back yard.

It was just two months before this day that we were messing around with boxing gloves.

Chapter Four

The Boxing Boys

Phillip's back yard was separated from the Lopez girls' house by a small, three-foot fence. Phillip's brother Jerry was two years older than he was. Jerry was one year older than I. On this evening there were a few of us at the Lopez girls' back patio listening to oldies.

The patio had a long bar that stretched all the way across the area. Behind it was a patch of green grass, with trees and bushes. We hung out there as long as their father Fred wasn't at home.

Fred was a man who liked to spend all of his time at the bar after work. Every evening he arrived home, and someone would shout out, "Fred's home!" Phillip, Bobby, Ray, Phillip's cousin, and I would dash over the fence to Phillip's house. The rest of the guys had to make their way to the back, over the fence, and into the field.

On this particular evening Phillip was called home by his mother for a few minutes before she and Manuel left the house. Besides us there were Henry, John, and Bert. We were messing around and talking. Also my sister Mildred and some other girls were there.

Phillip came outside, holding a pair of boxing gloves. "Hey, who wants to box?" he yelled out with his adventurous smile.

"Hey, Phillip, I do," Ray answered as he stood.

"All right, Ray! Come on. You think you can beat me?" Phillip asked.

We would mess around with his boxing gloves every so often. We got a kick out of it, saying we were practicing for our street fights.

Ray stepped over the small fence to Phillip's yard. They put on the gloves. Phillip was looking at his cousin as he was putting on his gloves.

"Ray, I'm going to wipe you out, man! You know, you don't stand a chance with me."

Ray was thin and about four inches taller than Phillip. He had a thin face with a long, thin nose. His complexion was on the dark side.

The rest of us stepped over the fence and sat on a brick fence around Phillip's patio. We wanted to see a good fight.

Ray smiled as Henry tied the strings on his gloves. He then said, "Oh yeah? I don't think so, small fry!"

Even though Phillip was short, he kept himself in shape. Jerry, Phillip's older brother, had a set of weights his mother and Manuel had bought him. Phillip and I worked out almost every day with them.

"Ready, Ray?" Phillip asked.

Ray was down on one knee having his glove tied. Phillip swung at Ray. The hit from Phillip's glove was more like a slap.

"Hey, man! I'm not ready yet!" Ray exclaimed, irritated.

"I am!" Phillip answered as he took another swing and hit Ray in the jaw, not too hard.

"Hey, man! That's no fair!" Ray yelled.

Ray stood and swung back, missing Phillip. All of us laughed. We egged Ray on to get Phillip back. Ray and Phillip were laughing at this point.

Boxing with the boys was a lot of fun. We never had a problem with one another or became angry with each other for hitting too hard. We knew we were boxing to give and to take hard punches. We knew that if we couldn't take it then we shouldn't put on the gloves.

Phillip and Ray danced around, warming up for the fight. They started to box. When they would hit each other hard, some of us gave a "Wow!"

They started to swing wildly at each other, both connecting at the same time and almost knocking each other out. We all started to laugh and egged them on even more. This was a good fight with a lot of action. When they both slowed down, we tried to convince Ray to charge Phillip. He wouldn't; he knew better.

In just a little while, Phillip announced it was someone else's turn. "I'm tired of hitting Ray so much! Who's next?"

Henry stood and said, "I'll go, Phillip. I know I can handle you easy. Give me the gloves, Ray."

Jerry, Phillip's brother, stepped out of the back door. He must have been in his bedroom. The bedroom window was facing the backyard. "Hey, I'll box."

Since Jerry was older then all of us, he thought he was tougher, which was far from the truth. Ray untied his gloves, shook them off, and said, "Not me, man!" He didn't want to fight with his older cousin.

"Come on, chicken!" Jerry teased.

I sat there and didn't say anything. I really didn't care for Jerry very much because he always tried to act like a big shot when he was with his friends. They were the kind of guys whose parents bought them new motorcycles. I thought of them as spoiled kids. Because Jerry was my good friend Phillip's brother, I never wanted to show him he really wasn't a big shot.

No one said anything. Phillip wasn't going to box with his older brother. Bobby, Henry, and Bert didn't move from where they were sitting. They were very quiet, not knowing if they could beat Jerry. They didn't want to look bad if they could avoid it. Besides, if they fought against someone they really didn't know well, they knew they might get angry. One thing could lead to another, and we would have a big problem with Phillip's brother.

"Come on, man! You guys are all chickens."

I really didn't want to box Jerry. This was a friendly game. Since I didn't really like Jerry, I knew I might become angry; and it wouldn't be a friendly fight anymore. He repeated, "You're all chickens!"

"OK, I'll box you, Jerry!" I answered as I stood, not appreciating being called a chicken. "But don't cry when we're done."

"Yeah, right, Arthur. Come on, I'll box you!"

Jerry didn't say too much more. I felt he really didn't want to box me. He would rather box one of the other guys. I had heard he was good at boxing with his group of friends; however, none of them were street fighters as we were.

I thought I was going to handle this really well and my prize would be getting Jerry good! I had always wished I could fight him. In junior high school, I had him in my class. He acted as if I were a young kid because I hung around with his little brother. He was just a little older than I. One time in school I almost fought him. We were just starting to dance around to fight when Mr. Jones, our teacher, stopped us.

"Are you ready, Jerry?" I asked once we both had our boxing gloves tied.

"Yeah, I'm ready. Throw your best shot, Arthur."

We started by dancing around slowly, giving each other a hard stare, concentrating. I saw his glove start to move to take a swing. I let go, moving very fast with a hard, left jab. Boom! Right on the forehead. Jerry brought his gloves in and close to his face, not having as much confidence anymore. I didn't want to egg him on because I wanted to knock him out right away.

Jerry threw a few more wild swings, thinking he was going to rile me up as he does his brother Phillip. He let his hands drop a bit, and I came in with my hard, right, knockout punch. There was nothing to stop it. Boom! This time it hit him square in the nose. He fell back and down on the grass.

"Hey! Man! Why do you have to hit so hard!" Jerry screamed. He shook off his gloves and held his nose as blood started to pour out of it. He picked up a rag that was lying over the bricks and held it against his nose, tilting his head back. He yelled again and said this wasn't fair. He was only playing, and I was really fighting. Everyone was quiet, knowing that if he kept yelling I might really become angry. Then there was going to be a real fight. Jerry's nose didn't want to stop bleeding.

"Man, I don't know why you hit me so hard! Now look what you've done! I was going to wear this shirt later!"

I felt like telling him to shut up and that he was a big crybaby. The only reason I didn't was because of my buddy Phillip. I knew I could have big problems with Jerry if I wanted; however, Manuel and his mother loved Jerry very much. They thought he was the greatest, and they felt Phillip was the troubled kid. If I made enemies with Jerry, it could cause problems with his brother and me hanging out.

Jerry went into the house to try to stop the bleeding. Bobby stood up and said happily, "All right, it's my turn! I'm going to teach you how to box, man!" Because everyone was quiet after what happened to Jerry, Bobby wanted to liven things up.

"Who do you want to box, Bobby or Henry?" I asked.

"No, I want to box the champ. If I beat you, then I will really look good. If I box Henry and win, that isn't anything!" he said jokingly.

Henry stood up and said laughingly, "Hey, man! I'll box you right now! I know you're no match for me!" Henry was a skinny guy. He looked like a bag of bones.

One of the Lopez girls, Margie, liked Henry; however, Phillip also liked Margie. Margie was playing around with both Phillip and Henry. She didn't know which one to be with when they we were all together at the same time.

"All right, Bobby. But you better block your nose, man!" I said, knowing more than likely Jerry was in his bedroom listening. Everyone started to laugh. They yelled out, "Watch that nose, Bobby!"

"Hey, man! I have a spare nose in my pocket. So if anything happens to this one, I'll just pull out my other one!" He laughed along with everyone else.

Bobby was all right. I didn't want to hurt him too badly. I wasn't planning on giving him a knockout punch. I just wanted to dance around and play with him. We both came out ready to fight. He took his first swing.

"Man, I love this boxing," I thought. The concentration and being able to strike with accuracy was so much fun. I jabbed Bobby and connected. He jabbed back. I jabbed a little harder, wanting him to feel it. I tried to get my punches in and out as fast as I could. He threw a few more at me as we danced around each other. I only threw my punches when I saw a slight opening.

Bobby threw a hard right, leaving himself open. I let go with a good, hard jab. I saw my glove hit his face between his eyes. His eyes rolled up, and his arms dropped. He froze where he was standing. I wasn't sure what was wrong with him. At first I thought he was playing. I knew I didn't hit him that hard. His eyes had a blank stare. I also let my arms drop. I looked at him and asked, "Bobby, you OK? Bobby?"

He didn't answer. Phillip, Henry, and Bert stood, recognizing something wasn't right.

Bobby's legs bent. He started to fall down to the ground. I reached out and caught him, not wanting him to be hurt as he fell to the ground. I laid him down gently, still thinking he was playing

around. "Bobby, knock it off, man!" I said, feeling really worried.
The guys stepped over to where we were. They all bent down to check Bobby. He seemed as if he were asleep.
Phillip was standing over him and said, "Hey, man. Hey, Bobby, you OK?"
We were all huddled around him. The girls from next door saw something was wrong. Sylvia called out, "What happened? Is something wrong?"
"It's Bobby. Arthur hit him hard and hurt him," Ray yelled back.
I felt really bad. I didn't think I hit him that hard and didn't know how he could be knocked out so easily.
As Sylvia came over the fence to see what happened, all the other girls and everyone else in the house also came outside and started to make their way over the fence to Phillip's back yard.
"What happened?" Margie asked, looking down at Bobby as Phillip was slapping his face and trying to wake him.
Bert had an expression on his face, as if the unbelievable had happened. Before answering Margie, he told Phillip, "Check to see if he's breathing. Maybe he's dead, man."
I felt my heart fall to my stomach. I really didn't mean to hurt my friend Bobby. I was trying to remove the gloves from my hands but couldn't because they were tied so tight. Henry saw me struggling and offered to help. "Let's see. I'll do it."
I extended my gloves out, so he could untie them. "Man, Arthur, why did you hit him so hard?" Henry asked.
I didn't answer, worried that maybe I killed Bobby.
"He's not waking up. Maybe we better call the ambulance. If we don't, he might die on us," Phillip said. Philip put his head down over Bobby's chest to listen to his heart. Everyone was quiet, waiting for the verdict. I was in deep thought, praying, "Please, God, don't let him be dead."
"Nope! He's alive! But we better call the ambulance."
Stella, the oldest of the Lopez girls, said, "I'll call." She turned and ran back to her house to telephone for the ambulance.
I bent down next to Bobby and said, "Hey, man? Hey, Bobby. Are you all right?"
I thought back to all the fun we had during our childhood years. I thought about the time, not so long ago, when we stole a car and

almost were caught three times in it. Bobby looked so funny when the cop was after him. We drove by where Bobby was hiding, and he came running out of some bushes to flag us down.

I sure hoped Bobby was going to be all right.

Within minutes I could hear the sirens racing toward us. It didn't sound like just one; it sounded as if there were a dozen emergency vehicles. I wondered if Stella had told them we were all hurt.

The noise of the sirens stopped as they approached the house. We were all quietly waiting. We heard voices coming around the house. Margie was standing where she could see down the side of Phillip's house. She looked our way and said, "It's the cops."

I thought, "The cops? What in the heck do they want? We need a doctor, not the cops!"

As they became visible to us, the first cop asked, "What happened here?"

Phillip started to answer. I could still hear more sirens approaching from far away. "My friends were boxing, and Bobby fell to the ground and didn't get up."

The cop looked down at Bobby as he lay there, still wearing his boxing gloves. "Who was boxing with him?" the cop asked.

"One of us was," Phillip answered, not wanting to get me into trouble. We never ratted to the cops on each other. We would rather go to Juvenile Hall than tell on someone. However, I didn't think this was a big deal to lie about. I wasn't trying to kill Bobby. We were just messing around. I didn't even hit him that hard and really didn't know what happened to him.

"Don't get smart with me, kid! I asked who was boxing with him?"

"I was," I answered, still shocked, thinking I might have really hurt Bobby.

Just then we heard the last siren come to a stop in front of the house. There were eight cops already there. The one cop told me to move to the other side of the lawn. When I stepped to where I was told, he asked me to turn around and hold up my hands. He frisked me to see if I had any weapons. I was directed to put my hands behind my back. He placed handcuffs on me. I felt the cold metal rap around my wrists, although the cop didn't put them on too tightly.

I heard talking from the side of the house and saw the ambu-

lance attendants come through the walkway with a stretcher.
The cop asked me, "What's his name?"
"Bobby Martinez."
"Do you know his phone number?"
"No, I don't. It's at home."
Phillip spoke up and said, "I have it. It's in the house." One of the other cops told Phillip to go and get it. When Phillip went in the house, the cop entered with him.

Another cop stepped into the back yard. He asked the cop who had handcuffed me, "What happened here?"

The cop turned to look at me as he answered, "Well, we have the boxing boys here. I think this one was really mad and took it out on that one." He was pointing at Bobby lying on the ground. The ambulance attendants were checking out Bobby's vital signs.

"Hey, how do you know? You didn't ask me anything about it. I didn't take anything out on anyone. Why would I want to do that? Bobby and me are friends, man!"

Just then the other cop came out of the house with Phillip. He was holding Jerry's rag. "Look what I found. The kid in the house said this is from his nose, but I don't think so. I think there is more here than meets the eye!"

The last cop to arrive must have been their boss. He told me, "OK, kid, come with me to the front."

As I stepped in front of him to walk out, Bobby was already on the stretcher and was being wheeled to the ambulance. I was right behind them.

The cop I was with turned and told the other cops who were standing around, "Find out what happened from the other boxing boys."

When we reached the street, I stopped to watch Bobby being placed in the ambulance, wishing he would wake up right then. I knew I was going to be very worried until he regained consciousness. I didn't want to be the one who killed him. I knew his mother and father would always hate me for it and didn't want this to happen.

I felt the cop's eyes observing me while I stood with my worried expression as the doors to the ambulance were being closed. In my mind I told Bobby, "Hey, kid, take care. I hope you're going to be all right, man."

"All right, over there to my car," the cop said as he pointed to one of the vehicles. As we were walking to it, he asked, "What is your name?"

"Art Rodriguez."

"Where do you live, Art?"

"Down the street. On this street."

I didn't know which police car was his. "Which car?" I asked.

"That one," he answered, pointing again.

It was now getting dark, and people from the neighborhood were standing around to see what happened. As we approached the car, the officer told me to stop where I was. I did. I felt him go down to my handcuffs. He removed them. I was relieved. This cop didn't speak hard as the other one in the back yard had spoken.

"Thanks, man." I muttered as I rubbed my wrist. I was glad they were off.

"All right, get in and have a seat in my office," he said as he opened the back door.

I obeyed. He closed the door. The door didn't have any handles for the window or to open it. I wanted to run home, but I knew it wouldn't be a good idea.

He opened the front door and sat in the driver's seat. I thought he was going to turn on the engine and take me to jail. Instead he lit a cigarette, took a long puff, turned his body halfway around, and put his arm over the seat. He blew out the smoke, sending it to the other side of the cop car. "All right, Art, tell me what happened."

"Nothing. We all said we were going to mess around with the boxing gloves. I was boxing with my friend Bobby, and I jabbed him with a left. That was it. I didn't even hit him hard."

"I understand you had an argument with him a little while ago. Or was that the other day?"

I thought this cop must have thought I was really stupid. I knew he had not talked to anyone yet. I knew for sure he was making this up as we spoke.

"What are you talking about? Who told you that? You just got here."

"I know I just got here, but I know what's going on in the neighborhood, Arthur. We know there was a shooting here not long ago. We are keeping an eye on you boys."

I figured he knew there was a shooting because he saw the reports the night Phillip and I were shooting off Manuel's shotgun. "Anyways, there was no argument. We're all good friends. That's the way it happened, just like I told you."

"Are you sure? Look, Art, I'll tell you what. I'll level with you. I have my officers back there right now finding out what really happened. If you tell me everything here and they come and tell me what I already know, I'll go easy with you. But if you want to play Mister Hard Guy, then it's not going to go well for you. Do you understand?" he questioned. He took another toke of his cigarette and blew out the smoke as if he were enjoying it. This cop was demanding but talking mildly.

"Look, officer, I'm telling you the way it was. There is nothing. Bobby is my friend, and we were boxing. Anyways, if we were really fighting, don't you think it's better to fight with gloves on than with knives?"

"Are you telling me you were angry with him, but you were handling it with gloves?"

I thought to myself, "Man, I said the wrong thing. Now this cop thinks I put something there so he could read in between the lines."

"No officer, I'm not saying that. Look, we were playing around; that's all. I hit Bobby, but not hard."

"What happened? You or he became angry?"

"No, he was knocked out. I hit him, and he went down. I didn't mean to hurt him."

"So that's why there was blood all over in the house?"

"No, I boxed with Phillip's brother Jerry; and I hit him in the nose. He started to bleed, so he stopped boxing."

"Are you sure you don't want to tell me anything else, Arthur?" he asked as he took another drag from his cigarette.

We stayed in the cop car going back and forth with same conversation. He would ask, "You were upset with Bobby, weren't you?"

I would answer, "No, we were messing around, I didn't try to hurt him!" The cop seemed as if he really didn't believe me.

Thirty-five minutes passed. The cop who placed the handcuffs on me came out to the front. The cop I was with saw him and told me, "I'll be right back."

He stepped out of the car and walked to the driveway, talking to the other officer for five minutes. I couldn't hear anything that was being said; however, I did see the cop I was with nodding his head as the other one did all the talking. The cop came back to the car and sat down again. "All right, Arthur. Why didn't you tell me about Jerry?" he asked, staring at me as if he found out something big.

"What about Jerry? I did tell you. You asked me about the blood, and I told you. We were boxing, and he got a bloody nose."

"You didn't tell me you were upset with him. Were you upset with him for something?"

"No, man! What's wrong with you guys. Can't we have fun and box? There's nothing wrong with boxing. We do it all the time. Would you rather we go out and steal cars or something else?" I asked, getting smart with the cop.

He sat there lost for words. He looked back at the other cop standing in front of the house, waiting for this cop to go and report what he found. He looked at me and said, "OK, Art." He stepped out of the side of the car and walked around to my side, opening the door. "Come on, get out."

I wondered where he was going to take me now. Once out of the car, he asked, "I might want to come back and talk to you. Where do you live again?" He took out a pad and pen.

I gave him the address. "On this street."

"OK, boxing boy. I want you to work hard and try to keep out of trouble." He then told me I was free to go.

The cop closed the door to his car and stepped over to the other officer. He told him to call the rest of the cops in the back yard to leave, and to get back to their duties in the streets. The other cop had an expression as if he didn't understand why they were leaving, feeling they could have made a bust.

Thirteen of us walked to San Jose Hospital to see how Bobby was doing. By the next day Bobby regained consciousness from a short coma. The doctors really didn't understand what happened to him. I was relieved I didn't kill my good buddy Bobby! Although he was knocked out this time, he didn't give up boxing.

Chapter Five

The Big Bandage

"Man, Phillip, this is a lot of beer! I don't think we are going to be able to drink very much of it," I said.

I had two bottles in a bag. Phillip had three bottles in his bag. Before leaving the house, we both took big gulps to hold us until we were in the clear on King Road.

We left Phillip's house and crossed the street. I looked back at the Lopez girls' house. "I wonder if anyone is up this early? Hey, man, maybe we should go to the back window to see if they want to come. What do you think?" I asked Phillip. Really, I wanted to show off and tell them we were going to the flea market to get high on our beer.

"Na, what if Fred wakes up? Then what?"

I was feeling the effects of the beer, looked at Phillip, and said laughingly, "So what, man? If he wakes up, then we'll do what we always do!"

"What's that?" Phillip asked.

"Yell out, 'Fred's home!'" We both broke out laughing.

"Then what, Arthur? Run?"

"No, man, I'm too smart for that. I know how much he likes beer. So I'll tell him he can have one of the bottles!" I bent over laughing. So did Phillip.

"Hey! Shh!" I said trying to stop laughing. "They are going to hear us out here, man! Let's not talk until we get on King Road. I think we're the only ones up this early in all of San Jose!"

Fred was a good man with me. I didn't know why, but he liked me. He had given me a job cutting his grass. He paid me $4.00 every week for the work. He never called me Arthur, always "boy."

King Road was a small country road. From Virginia Place to San Antonio Street was a field with tall grass next to the road. Between the field and the road ran an old barbed-wire fence. We were talking as we walked. A little way down the road, Phillip said, "Hey, let's stop here and rest. That way we can have a drink of our beer."

"That sounds good to me."

The fence was down at this spot. We walked twenty feet into the field. The grass was three feet tall and still green. We sat down and couldn't be seen by the passing cars, which were not very many at that time in the morning.

I took out one of my bottles and took a big swallow. "Ah, this is good, man! How did you get such a good idea, Phillip?"

"I don't know how I did it. We have enough to last until tonight. I think I'm going to stay out all day and all night. My mom and Manuel will have a big hangover from all they drank, and they'll never know."

"We should've stopped at the girls' house. They would've got a kick out of it," I said, disappointed.

"Yeah, but what the heck, man, we're going to have a good time anyways."

"Hey, Phillip, remember I cut my foot a few months after I met you?"

"Oh, yeah, man. You couldn't wear a shoe. I remember that. I really didn't know you then. What happened anyways," Phillip asked, lying down on the grass with one arm holding up his head and the other holding onto his bottle.

"Listen to this, man. It's really funny. I was home alone that day, and I was sharpening this stick with a big knife from the kitchen."

Phillip cut in, "Why? What were you going to use it for?"

"I don't know, man. All I remember is that I was sharpening it, maybe to fight with Eddie. I don't know. Anyways, I was sharpening the stick and sitting like this," I explained as I sat with my legs crossed in an Indian position. "I was going like this with the knife." I acted as if I had a knife in my hand, sharpening an invisible stick. Phillip was lying on the ground laughing as I acted out what I was doing. "Then the knife slipped, and I cut the bottom of my foot right here, man." I pointed to the bottom of my foot under my big toe.

"Wow, Arthur! You're joking! How big was the cut?"

"It was big, man! It was bleeding like heck. And remember I was the only one home. I didn't know what to do!"

"Did it hurt?" Phillip asked, squelching his eyes as if he felt it.

"Heck, yeah, it hurt. What do you think? Man, did it hurt. I think it went in deep. I know it was this long," I said, forming a three-inch width with my fingers.

"Man! What did you do?"

"Now we're going to get to the funny part!"

"Funny? You mean there's a funny part to this?"

"Heck, yeah, or else I wouldn't be telling you all this. So anyways, I didn't know what to do. I got a towel and held it against the cut. But I don't think it did any good. The towel got all red with blood in no time."

"So what did you do?" Phillip wanted me to speed up the story.

"I called down the Lopez girls' house to see if my mother was there. She wasn't. So I told Sandy what happened." Sandy was the youngest of the Lopez girls. I continued, "She asked how bad it was bleeding. I told her it was bleeding really bad. She told her father. Fred told the girls to go to my house to see if it was really bad."

"Really? That was pretty good of Fred."

"Yeah, he likes me. I don't know why. He has always liked me. I don't know why I run when he gets home. I should stay one of these days and see what he says."

"No way, man! He'll probably think you want to marry one of the girls!" We both laughed.

"Na, I don't think so. He knows Tita my sister is Sandy's best friend."

"Yeah, he does. Maybe you should stay and not run one of these days! But what if he throws you out the window? I stay all the time," Phillip said. "Anyways, what happened when the girls went to your house?"

"Well, they saw all the blood that was coming out of my cut and were really worried. I think from the expressions they had they thought I was going to die with all the blood that was in the bathroom. So they called Fred and told him I was bleeding, and the bleeding wouldn't stop. I heard his voice on the phone from where I was. He was talking loud. He said, 'Get that boy over here right now! I want to see how bad he cut himself.'"

"Really? Wow," Phillip replied as he took another big gulp of his beer. I guzzled a few swallows also. I was having fun sitting in the tall grass with the fragrance of a summer morning all around me. As I was recouping from drinking so much beer at once, I heard a few cars and what sounded like a big truck pass.

"Anyways, where was I? Oh, yeah, I hopped all the way to the girls' house. I had one arm over Sandy and the other over Margie. When they got tired, Stella and Sylvia took over helping me. When we got to their house, Fred was waiting at the front door. He was frowning as if he were angry or something. He looked at us and with a mild voice said, 'Bring the boy into the bathroom. Be careful with him. Without him we'll never get our lawn mowed!'"

"Na, he didn't say that, did he?"

"No. Not about the lawn. I was just throwing that in to liven things up!" We both laughed again.

"Go on. What happened next?"

"I sat on the edge of the tub, and Fred removed the bloody towel. All four girls were at the doorway looking to see what their father was going to do. Once he pulled off the towel that was covered with blood, he said, 'Gees! What in the heck did you do, boy? Were you fighting with someone? How did they get you on the bottom of your foot?' I didn't know what to say. I told him I was sharpening something, and the knife slipped. That is what happened. I don't think he believed me."

"Why didn't he believe you?"

"I don't know. It just seemed to me that he didn't believe me. Then when he took off the towel, the blood was still pouring out of my cut. It didn't want to stop bleeding. He turned and told one of the girls to get the tape from the medicine cabinet in the bathroom. Margie handed him the tape. Fred then turned and looked around the bathroom, and guess what he did?"

Phillip sat up and wanted to know. "I don't know, what?"

"Guess, man! If you don't try to guess, I'm not going to tell you!" I insisted as I laughed.

Phillip was thinking. As he thought, I took another big drink of my beer. The effect of the beer was getting to me pretty strongly at this point.

"Get another towel? I don't know. That's the only thing I can think of."

"Well, get this. He told Stella to hand him the box of Kotex!"

Phillip broke out laughing, not believing it. "No, man! You're kidding? That is really funny! What did the girls say or do?"

"They all stood there with their hands over their mouths in disbelief. They didn't know if their father was serious. Man, I'm telling you, you should have seen them!"

Phillip couldn't stop laughing. He was rolling on the grass, holding his stomach. "Man, I can't believe Fred did that! Then what happened?" he asked as he regained his composure.

Just as I was going to tell Phillip, a car pulled over a few feet from where we were. "Hey, who is that? A cop? Hide the beer!" I said.

Phillip put the beer behind him. I stooped down. The people in the car couldn't see us, and we couldn't see them. Phillip also went down, and we didn't move. We sure didn't want a cop to catch us with the beer. We were already high as it was. I knew if it was a cop, I was going to take off running through the field as fast as I could.

I looked over at Phillip. He was still holding his hand over his mouth, trying to stop laughing at the thought of Fred wanting to use the Kotex on my foot with the girls present.

We heard someone get out of the car. In a few minutes they got back in, the car door slammed shut, and they drove away. Phillip said, "Man, I'm sure glad it wasn't the cops. I don't know if I could run fast enough right now. Go on, tell me what happened with Fred."

"Do you think we should leave? What if someone reports us here with the beer?"

"They don't know we have beer," Phillip said, laughing.

"Yeah, OK. Anyways, Stella didn't move. She was in shock!"

Phillip started laughing again. He thought it was so funny. "Why would he do that? I can't believe it!"

"But, hey, man, my foot was still bleeding! He had to do something. There wasn't anything else around."

"And what happened?"

"Fred yelled at Stella again and told her, 'I said get the Kotex! Hurry!' Then she reached for them, even though she didn't want to. I think she would have rather seen me bleed to death!" I said jokingly, laughing at the same time.

"Wow, Arthur, that must have been funny."

"It was, but I couldn't laugh. Fred was my doctor at the time and was trying to help me. He wrapped four Kotexs on my foot, taping them. He taped them on tight. I thought I was going to die because they were on so tight. Then he told me to leave them on for at least a day."

"That is really funny. Did you leave them on for a day?"

"No. When my father got home, he saw them taped to my foot and laughed. He wanted to know why I used them. I told him Fred put them on me."

"What did your father do?"

"He took them off and bandaged me up right, with real first aid stuff. I really didn't want them on my foot anyway, man! You know what I mean?" I said as I took another drink of beer.

"Yeah, I know. Hey, we better get going. We have a long way to walk," Phillip replied as he took one more swallow of his beer.

I drank a little more than half of my bottle. We stood up in the tall grass and started walking again. Phillip looked toward the field as he picked up the bag of beer and asked, "I wonder who owns the field out there?"

I thought back to the incident of the cherry bomb.

Chapter Six

The Cherry Bomb

On Virginia Place fields surrounded us. Behind us the field belonged to the Prusch family which they used for dairy cows. As the years went by, a trailer court was built on part of the Prusch family's land behind our house.

At the end of the street was the field that went to Highway 101; Today it is a freeway. Back then there were signal lights at 101 and Story and 101 and San Antonio. Next to the highway was a large swamp with a bamboo jungle. During the summer months we would build rafts and float in the water on the swamp, two feet deep.

Once in a while I would fall off the raft and sink in a foot of stinky mud at the bottom of the swamp. I would join Eddie and our friends on Virginia Place and catch frogs, as well as what looked like small fish.

Water would stay in the swamp all year long. During the summers we would take our shovels to dig and set up our forts in the fields next to the swamp. We spent most of our summer days in the fields playing, having rock battles in our forts. We would even take our canned food and build a small fire to warm it. Our forts were dug two feet in the ground. Then we would build three-foot walls all around and make an opening to pass in and out. We even built roofs on them. The guys from our block would go to the fort every day until we tired of it. When that happened we would tear it down and construct a new and better fort on a different spot in the field.

On one hot summer morning, I was with Eddie in the back yard turning over dirt. I was eight years old. Our father had dump trucks dump 15 piles of fill in our yard because every time the Prusch Ranch would water the field our backyard flooded, which was all the time. We had to work at least two or three hours before we were allowed to have fun with our friends. Eddie and I always arose early in the morning before it became too hot.

"Hey, Eddie and Arthur," Donald greeted us as he came to the back yard. "Are you guys almost done?"

Donald lived a few houses down the block across the street. He was a short guy with a round face. Donald is Chicano; however, his eyes made him appear oriental.

"Yeah, we are," Eddie answered. "Why? What's up?"

"Fernando and Richard are coming too. They want to build a fort in the field behind our houses where that mean guy lives."

I was standing with the shovel handle under my jaw, holding my head up straight. I asked, "Why? Why don't we make our fort in the other field? If the man doesn't like us, why bother there? There are lots of other places we can make a fort."

The man who lived in the lone house in the field always gave us dirty looks when we walked by his place. We knew he didn't like us very much, although he had never told us anything about playing in the field around his house.

Donald answered, "Well, we're not going to build it by his house. We want to build it farther into the field."

Just as Donald was speaking, Gene came walking from the side of the house to the backyard. Gene was a kid who lived on Virginia Place, a few houses away and across the street from us. His family was from Oklahoma. They had a strong southern accent. Gene had blonde hair and was on the thin side. "Hey, are they coming, Donald? Hey, Eddie and Arthur, are you guys coming? Are you almost done working?" Gene asked.

"Eddie, I think we're done. What do you think?" I asked, tired of spreading dirt. It seemed as if we had been working on the dirt for months and never achieved anything.

Eddie looked at the work we had done. He was trying to picture our father looking at it when he arrived home and wondered how he would view our work.

"I don't know. I think Dad wanted us to do more. Maybe we should come back later and do more work, just in case he doesn't like what we did."

I let my shovel fall where I was standing. If Eddie said I was done, then I was done. He was my big brother and knew more than I did. "Let's go. I'm ready," I stated.

"Hi, Eddie," greeted Fernando as he walked toward us with his younger brother Richard behind him.

"Hi, Fernando," I responded even though he wasn't greeting me.

I liked Fernando. He had always been all right with me and other younger kids in the neighborhood. He would even give the younger kids money, never wanting any favors in return. He liked being nice to people. Fernando was the kind of guy who always liked to look clean and neat. Even when we were in the fields, he looked as if he didn't get dirty.

"Hi, Arthur, are you done? Are you coming with us to the field?"

"Hey, Fernando and Richard," Eddie greeted.

"Yeah, I'm going. Right now?" I asked.

"Yeah, bring your shovel. We're going to need it."

Donald picked up a shovel also. So did Gene. Richard asked where the picks were so that he could get the hole started for our new, cool fort.

Richard had a dark complexion. Through the years some people thought Eddie and Richard were brothers because they were both thin and tall. They both had thin noses. Eddie had straight hair, and Richard had wavy hair.

We all walked out to the front of our house to the street. We went to the end of Virginia Place and around the back of the houses that were across the street from my house. We passed some walnut trees right behind the houses and then walked a few hundred feet into the field.

"Hey, you guys. I think this will be a cool place for our fort. There's no trees in our way, so we can see all the way to the other side of the field. If anyone comes, we'll spot them right away," Donald stated, looking at all of us to see what we thought.

We always wanted a clear view from all sides, just in case the guys from other neighborhoods came and wanted to do battle with us in a rock fight. We always wanted to be ready for a good fight. Once we built our fort, we would stock pile it with rocks.

We all stopped and looked around. Fernando was the oldest of all of us. He picked up his shovel and struck it into the ground. "This is good," he said as he looked over toward the man's house about a block away, the man who didn't like us very much.

I also looked in that direction. It appeared no one was home. "Good! Right here!" I declared as I started digging.

We all labored on our fort for the rest of the day. Some of us went back to our houses to look for lumber for the walls and the roof. Time went by fast. Before we knew it, it was late.

By the afternoon we were done. We had dug two feet down, ten-by-ten feet square. We had even made a small barbecue pit inside of the fort with an opening for the smoke to escape. We thought it really looked cool.

Eddie looked at me and said, "Hey, Arthur, we better get home. Dad should be getting home anytime now!" I dropped my shovel and felt a chill come over me. I hoped my father wasn't home yet.

"We'll be back in the morning, you guys. We have to get home," Eddie told everyone. He looked at me and said, "We better go, Arthur, cause if Dad gets home and finds we're not there working, he'll have a fit!" We left our shovels there because we had extras at home.

Donald looked at us and knew what he meant. "OK, I'll go over later. Hope your dad is in a good mood."

Upon arriving home, we saw our father's car in the driveway. "Man, I knew we should have left earlier," Eddie declared, disappointed.

I looked at the house to see what Eddie was looking at. I also saw the car. "Oh, no! I sure hope he's in a good mood."

We made our way around to the back yard to see if our father was inspecting our work yet. As we were going around the side, we could already smell my mother's cooking and her tortillas. It sure smelled good.

Everything was quiet, and there was no sign of Dad. We entered the back door of the house. I saw Mom next to the stove making tortillas. Dad's customary sitting place at the kitchen table was still not visible from where I was. Eddie and I took a few more steps toward our bedroom. We hoped our father wasn't in the kitchen. We had to pass the hot water heater and then the kitchen threshold. We both moved slowly and quietly. Just as we were stepping by the kitchen threshold, Dad spoke up, "Edmundo! Arturo! Where were you?"

I looked at Eddie for him to give the answer because he was

always so good at it. Only once in a while we would be beaten for something he said wrong. I would always say the wrong thing to our father. It didn't go well for us when I spoke.

"We were at Fernando's house, Dad. We did the work you wanted us to do today. We did a lot."

"I saw what you did," he said with a stern voice. "It was not very much. I wanted you to do more."

"I know, Dad, but the ground was hard. It was really packed in there."

Dad's eyes scanned both our bodies up and down. He saw we were really dirty with dirt. He must have figured we labored really hard in the back yard, and the ground must have been packed down just as Eddie said. "OK, go take a fast shower! Supper is almost done!"

My mother turned as we were walking away and said, "Don't take too long, boys!"

"OK, Mom, we won't," I answered, relieved that everything went well with Dad.

We took our fast showers and were done just in time for supper, remaining in our room. We didn't want to come out unless we had to. Our bedroom door opened.

"Arthur, Eddie, Mom said supper is ready! Come and eat!" Tita our little sister yelled, even though she was at our open bedroom door.

"OK, Tita! You don't have to yell. We can hear you!"

"Dad said to call you, and that's what I'm doing! So come and eat!"

"OK. OK, man! Hold your horses!"

Tita went running to the kitchen, yelling, "Mom, Arthur said, 'hold your horses!'"

"Ay, Tita, sit down at your place!" I heard Mom declare.

As we left our bedroom, we could smell the chicken mole and the homemade tortillas. As we were nearing the kitchen, I told Eddie, "Hey, Eddie, wouldn't it be cool if Mom would come to one of our forts and cook there?"

Eddie looked at me as if I were crazy, "Yeah, right, Arthur!"

We all sat at the table at our places. Sometimes our father, mother, Tita, and baby brother Victor would eat first. Then Eddie and I would eat. Dad sat at his place at the end of the table. As we were taking our seats, Mom was putting the last things on the table before she sat next to my father. We waited until we were told we could serve ourselves. We didn't say very much at the dinner table. My mother and father would speak Spanish most of the time. Mom would answer Dad in English and speak a little in Spanish.

"What did you boys do today while you were gone?" my mother asked.

I spoke up, wanting to talk to Mom. "Well, first we went to Fernando's house. Then we went to the field and built a fort."

Eddie's foot kicked me a little. I didn't know what was wrong with him and didn't think I said anything I should not have said. I continued, "It was really neat. We dug two feet down, so we can hide in the fort."

Dad was taking it all in as we spoke. He thought we were dirty because of all the work we did in the back yard. Eddie gave me an expression which said, "Shut up, Arthur!" I still didn't know why he looked at me in that way; however, I soon found out.

"Ah! You did not do much trabajo (work) here, but you went to the field and did it there? What's the matter with you? I gave you a trabajo (work) to do. I should spank you for trabajando (working) in the field and not trabajando aquí (working here)!"

Mom interrupted, "Was it shady there, Arthur?"

I knew what my mother was doing. At times she would say things to distract my father when he was getting upset, although she didn't do it very often.

"Yeah, it was."

"Who did you go with?" Mom asked. I was waiting for Eddie to jump into the conversation; but he didn't want to, since I placed myself in this jam by sticking my foot in my mouth.

"Well, it was Fernando, Richard, Donald, and Gene."

"Was it all right with Richard's mother that you were digging in the field?" she asked.

Fernando and Richard's parents didn't care what they did during the day. We were the only ones who had so much work to do at home.

My father didn't say anything. He wanted to see what I was going to say about their parents. What my mom did worked. Now my father was sidetracked.

"Yeah, his mom said it was all right if we played in the field. They did most of the work. We were tired from all the work we did here. So they worked hard there." I answered, hoping Dad would take into consideration that they did most of the work.

For the rest of our supper, my mom did most of the talking in Spanish. We ate our food and asked if we could leave when we were done.

"Yes, but go and work in the back for an hour," my father said, wanting us to pay for digging in the field instead of in our yard.

The next morning we arose early, looking forward to going to our new fort. We wanted to do as much work as possible that our father required. In two hours, at about 9 a.m., Donald came around to the back yard. "Hey, you guys ready?"

Eddie looked at me and stated, "Let's go. This is enough!"

We dropped our shovels and walked away from our work. Donald said, "Hey, take some food. We can cook there."

"I'll get some," I replied.

"Hey, don't worry about a can opener, I have one there. We took a lot of stuff already."

As we approached the fort, Gene, Richard, and Fernando were there, gathering small pieces of wood from under the walnut trees nearby. They were also gathering rocks just in case we needed them.

Someone had brought a grill to put over the fireplace we dug. Someone else brought some pots to heat up the food.

"Hey, I have a can of beans in here," Gene said as he pulled out the can from the big paper bag.

Richard was trying to light the wood in the fire pit but couldn't get it started. "I need some paper to start this off," he declared.

Donald emptied his big paper bag and handed it to Richard. "Here, you can use this one."

I also took everything out of my paper bag and handed it to Richard.

"Hey, here's some newspaper I found outside too," Gene offered.

"Good," Richard said. "All this will work!"

The fire started. The wood was very dry. Richard stood back as the fire grew quickly. "Hey, man, I think we put too much wood in here!" Richard yelled. Actually it was all the paper that was making the fire grow so fast.

The fire really became big and looked as if it were going to set all the wood in the fort on fire. Richard yelled out, "Man, we are going to be killed in here! Let's get out fast!" The smoke was getting really bad in the fort, and the fire was getting bigger by the second.

Eddie, Fernando, and Gene were outside gathering more wood when they heard Richard yelling; they turned to see what was happening. They saw all the smoke shooting out from the roof. From inside the fort the fire wasn't as big as it seemed from the outside. We didn't know if we should get out of the fort or stay inside. "Hey, I hope it don't catch the walls on fire. Then the whole field is going to burn!" I yelled.

Donald yelled out, "Get something to put it out before it gets too big!"

Just then Gene came down the little ramp we had dug to be able to enter the fort quickly. He had a flat board to hit the fire. By this time it was burning down; therefore, Gene didn't have to hit the fire much to try to put it out.

"Man, that was a close one," Richard declared. "I'm glad it didn't burn the whole field!"

At that moment the fire was burning at the right height. Donald started to open a can of beans when we heard a man's voice outside. "Hey, boys! What do you think you are doing here?"

I looked out of a crack in the wall and saw the mean man who lived in the only house in the field. Fernando answered, "Nothing, just playing. We built a fort and are going to play in it. Why?"

"A fort? What happened? Did the Indians start a fire? No. No. No. No fort here! You boys go home. You can't play here!" the man demanded harshly.

"But we ain't bothering anyone. What's it to you if we have a fort here?" Gene asked.

"What's it to me? You almost burned down my house! That's what it's to me! Now go home right now, or I'll call the cops on you!"

Richard came out of the fort, followed by Donald and me. "Hey, you can't tell us to leave. This isn't your property!" Richard stated.

"If you boys aren't out of here really fast, the cops will be here! Now get!"

"Man!" I exclaimed. "After all this work!"

I went back down into the fort and picked up my stuff. Everyone else started to complain as they also went in to gather their things.

The man stood there smoking his cigarette as we all were getting ready to leave.

As we walked away, we turned to look at him. Richard said, "That dumb old man. He's a jerk." Everyone made similar comments loud enough so that he could hear us. We made our way back to Richard's house and sat on his picnic table in his back yard.

What do you guys want to do?" Fernando asked.

"Let's blow up his house," Gene advised.

"Hey, that sounds like a good idea. Why don't we?" Richard said, perking up. "I have a cherry bomb left over from the 4th of July. I was saving it for a rainy day! I think the rainy day is here!"

"Hey, yeah!" Gene said happily. "Let's do it!"

Eddie agreed with Gene and replied, "The guy deserves it, but when should we do it?"

I was the youngest; therefore, I thought I would leave all these big decisions to the older guys. It sounded as if it would be fun to blow up the mean man's house.

"Tonight," Fernando answered. "But it has to be late, when everyone is asleep. We don't want anyone to see us."

"Good idea!" Richard answered. "Let's all meet here at 9:30 tonight. How do you think we should do it?"

"Let's put it by his front door and knock on the door. Then when he comes out, we'll scare the heck out of him!" Donald declared.

"But what if he steps on it?" Gene wanted to know.

Richard answered, "Then we can go back to our fort because he won't be able to go and tell us anything anymore!"

We all laughed. Richard looked over at me as he laughed because I wasn't saying anything. I was excited, thinking I was going to have fun with the older guys that night.

I thought, "I sure hope we don't get caught. If Dad knew what we were going to do, he would kill us for sure!"

We all went home and planned to meet back at Richard's house at 9:30 p.m. All evening I wondered how it was going to go when we lit the cherry bomb. At 9 o'clock sharp Eddie told me he was going to ask Dad if we could go to Richard's house. (During the summer months we were allowed to stay out late. San Jose was a quiet town, and nothing really bad happened to kids.)

Dad was lying on the sofa in the living room with his head on my mother's lap watching TV. "Dad, is it OK if me and Arthur go to Richard and Fernando's house?"

"What are you going to do there so late?" Dad asked as he lifted his head to look at Eddie.

"I don't know, Dad, play hide and seek or something."

"OK, but you guys better not be malcriados (bad kids)! If you are, you are going to pay for it! Ha, ha, ha," my father sang as he gave his sarcastic laugh. We knew what this meant. We knew that if we did do something bad we better make sure we didn't get caught.

As we were leaving the house through the back door, I said to Eddie, "Man, Eddie, I hope we don't get caught for this. Because if we do, then . . ."

"Hey, Arthur, if you don't want to go, then stay home. You don't have to come!"

"No, I want to go. I'm just saying . . ."

"Well then, quit crying about it. If we get caught, we get caught! That's it." I didn't say anything more until we arrived at Richard's house.

By the time we arrived everybody else was waiting. Some were sitting, and some were standing around the picnic table under the patio. The patio was away from the house, and there was a small house next to the patio where no one lived. "What took you guys so long?" Donald asked.

Eddie answered, "What do you mean what took us so long? We said 9:30, and it's not even 9:30 yet."

"Yeah, but we have to have a plan!" Donald replied.

He looked at Fernando and asked, "OK, how are we going to do this? I can't wait to get that old man back!"

Fernando looked at his brother and asked, "You got the cherry bomb, right? Let's see it."

Richard took out a little bag he was hiding under his shirt. He dumped it out on the table. The cherry bomb was with smaller firecrackers. It was really big! Compared to the other firecrackers, it seemed as if it would be able to blow up the whole house. It really looked like a bomb. I wondered how much noise it was going to make.

"Here you go, Fernando. This should keep that old man off our backs!"

Fernando took the cherry bomb and held it up close to his face.

"Yeah, I think this is going to do it. First we'll go to the field and hide for a little while. We'll make sure no one is around to tell on us. We sure don't want to get caught blowing up the old man's house. Then we'll sneak up to the house, put the bomb on his porch, knock on his door, and run like mad! And I mean fast, man!" We all started laughing. This was very exciting for us.

When we had the plan well in our minds, we moved out of the patio area, heading toward the field. It was very dark behind the houses. We stopped about three hundred feet from the man's house. The tall grass was about two feet high and very dry. We stayed there for a bit, not saying anything, just checking things out. We saw lights on inside the man's house and could see someone moving around through the curtains. We were very still. All around us we heard crickets singing. The sky was clear. Every little while we saw a shooting star. It was neat being out in the field at this time of night.

"Hey, you guys," Richard whispered, "We should get one of those shooting stars to hit the house!" We all started laughing.

"Yeah, man," Donald said as he made a noise with his lips, blowing them and making a spitting sound. He made a motion with his hand as if it were a shooting star coming down and heading for the man's house. "BOOM!" he exclaimed. We all started laughing again.

The front door opened, and the man appeared. He heard us outside and stood there for a few seconds. We all squatted down a bit and didn't move. If he would have started to walk toward us, we all knew exactly what we were going to do. Run!

"Hey! Who's out here? You better go home, or I'm going to get my gun and shoot you! Get out of here!"

I thought the guy sounded really scary and mean and deserved to be blown up with our cherry bomb.

The man stood there for thirty seconds trying to listen for any noises. No one even breathed. He then turned and went back into his house, slamming the door behind him. We still didn't say anything, thinking maybe he was peaking out of his window. Or maybe there was a back door, and he went out the back to try to come around quietly to catch us. We lay in the tall grass, lifting only our heads to scan the area. Nobody said anything, not knowing if the old, mean man snuck out the back door.

"Shh," Fernando whispered with his finger up to his lips. "Does anyone see anything? I thought I heard a noise coming from the other side of the house."

We were all wide-eyed, hoping the man wasn't on the other side of the house. We didn't want him to shoot us when we were planning to blow up his house.

I spoke up. "I don't see anything. I think he's in the house. Hey, I'm ready when you are, Fernando."

"OK, you guys, let's go. But you have to be quiet. We don't want him to come out again."

We all crawled through the tall grass very slowly, making our way to the wooden porch. Once there, we stood. Fernando took the cherry bomb out of his pocket. "OK, Eddie, you can knock when we tell you. I'll light it."

Fernando put the cherry bomb in the center of the porch. Richard took the matches out of his pocket. He was standing on the other side of the porch from where I was. The night was very dark, even there by the house. Richard tore a match from the book of matches and warned, "OK, everyone, get ready to run. I'm going to light it."

Richard placed the match next to the striking part of the book of matches. He was ready. He looked at me as if he were saying, "Get ready, Arthur! Run as fast as you can!"

Just at that instant, a noise came from the door. We both ducked down as fast as we could. Donald and Gene were on my side. They were already down on the ground. Richard, Fernando, and Eddie were down on the other side of the small porch. I squatted down but couldn't get all the way down or the man would have seen me as he opened the door. I froze. The wooden porch was made of 2 by 4's with big cracks or openings between them. I saw the man step out on the porch, looking out toward the field.

"Hey, you kids!" he yelled, "I said, get home! I'm going to call the cops on you! But if I catch you first, I'm going to bring you into my house and beat the heck out of you! Then I'll bury you in the back of my house! Get out of here, and go home while you have a chance!"

I was waiting for him to look down. If he would have, he would have seen me as well as all the other guys. He stood there as I looked up at him. I saw his big, ugly nostrils. "Man, he looks ugly," I thought. He looked even uglier from where I was. I was watching him because if he was to look down, I, as well as everyone else, was going to make our getaway as fast as we could. I had the urge to start running right at that moment.

"Don't forget," he yelled, "If I come out there and catch you, you're going to regret it! He turned around and went back into the house and slammed the door behind him again. As the door slammed, I heard him say, "Darn kids! I'll kill them!"

None of us moved a muscle for a few moments. We were in shock because we were almost caught.

In two minutes Fernando stood up, and then Richard, Eddie, Donald, and Gene also stood. I didn't know if I should. Richard again took his match and was ready to strike it. Eddie reached over the porch and was ready to bang on the door. Richard struck the match; it didn't light. I almost started running early. If I would have, the man might have heard me, coming out to catch everyone else. Richard struck the match again; this time it lit. He moved the match to the cherry bomb, and it lit. Eddie banged hard on the door four times, and we all started running as fast as we could. I didn't know if the cherry bomb actually lit, but I wasn't taking any chances.

I ran as fast and hard as I could, seeing Richard and Donald running behind me. Because I was the youngest and the smallest, I saw them, as well as Eddie, Gene, and Fernando, pass me and leave me behind. The fence was approaching, and I was ready to leap over it as soon as I reached it. I saw everyone in front of me go over it. Then I heard noise behind me.

I imagined the old man stepping out onto the porch and on the cherry bomb with his rifle in his hands, aiming at my back. I was waiting for a gunshot to go off and then feel a pain in my back. I was scared, but at the same time I was thrilled because it was exciting. I went over the fence behind someone's house! I rolled on the ground a few times, jumped to my feet, and kept right on running as fast as I could. As I went around the side of the house to the front, I saw all the guys on the sidewalk walking, circling each other out of breath, clapping their hands together and slapping their hands on their thighs, trying to talk as they caught their breath. They all turned to look at me. I wondered why the cherry bomb didn't ignite. At that moment I heard a giant BOOM!

Chapter Seven

The Drowning

"Hey, Arthur, why are you so quiet? Want to stop and take another drink of beer?" Phillip asked. We were approaching San Antonio Street.

"Yeah, I'll have a drink. I was just thinking back to when I was a kid. We lit a cherry bomb on some old man's porch."

"Oh yeah, you were saying something about that back there. What happened? Did you kill the guy with a cherry bomb?"

We stopped at the corner and sat on a fence by a house. "I don't know what happened to the guy. We put the cherry bomb there and heard it go off. But we never heard anything more about it. I know it didn't kill the guy because we saw him around later. But I do know this. He never bothered us again."

"Cool, Arthur, sometimes that's what it takes, a cherry bomb!" Phillip said as he laughed.

We had our drink of beer, both really feeling the effects and were not walking very straight. Phillip wanted to stop at Henry's house to see if he wanted to go with us. Henry lived on the corner of King Road and St. James Street. We walked up to his door and knocked hard. His mother came to the door and in Spanish asked what we wanted. We asked for Henry. She was a very old lady; Henry's father looked very old also. We didn't know if they were really old or had a hard life. Some people who came from Mexico grew old fast.

"No esta," Henry's mother said.

"OK, bye, Señorita," Phillip replied. We walked to the sidewalk and continued down King Road toward the flea market.

"Hey, Phillip, aren't you supposed to call young ladies señoritas and old ladies señoras?"

"I don't know, man. What's the difference?"

"Well, she is an old lady. Maybe you offended her by calling her a señorita, man."

"I don't think so. I think I probably made her feel good cause she probably thought I thought she looks really young, and that's why I called her señorita."

We had another friend who lived one street from Henry. We thought at first we wanted to invite him to go with us to the flea market, but we decided not to ask him. When we reached Alum Rock Avenue, we stopped and sat at the bus stop to rest.

"Man, I'm tired already, Arthur!" Phillip declared as he flopped down on the bench.

"I think it's the beer that is making us tired. We walk a lot farther than this all the time."

"I know, like walking to Alum Rock Park. I feel like going to Alum Rock Park, don't you? We should go there and go swimming."

Alum Rock Park had a big indoor swimming pool with a large slide on the side of it. It also had two regular diving platforms and one high dive. The park is located in the foothills of San Jose. It is a valley carved out of the Diablo Mountain range and has many oak trees, with a lot of green grass, picnic tables, and barbecue pits.

"I don't think so, man; it's too far. We already had plans to go to the flea market. Hey, did you tell Tom we were going to his tire shop there? Does he know?" I asked.

"Heck, no! He don't care if we go. I always go to his place." As Phillip said this, the county bus pulled up to where we were sitting. "Last chance. You sure you don't want to go up there?" The county buses went all the way up Alum Rock Avenue and into the park.

"No, I don't want to go. I would rather go to the flea market. There'll be girls there."

"Hey, boys, you getting on or not?" the fat bus driver yelled.

"No, we're only resting, Mister, thanks."

The bus door closed, and the bus moved away. I took a drink of my yellow Coke. I hoped that if anyone saw me drinking it they would think it was yellow Coke.

"Hey Phillip, I remember when I was a kid, maybe seven years old. We were at Alum Rock Park. I think it was Easter Sunday. There were a lot of people there. We had just got off the swings. Remember all the kids that went there then?"

"No. Remember, I'm not from here. I'm from Visalia, down south. I've been to Alum Rock Park a lot now that we moved here but not when I was a kid. Anyway, what happened?"

"Well, there were a lot of kids playing. Eddie and I just got off the swings, as I said, and were walking to where my dad and mom were lying on the grass when we heard people yelling and screaming."

"Yeah? What happened? Did someone die?" Phillip asked, kidding.

"Yeah, man. It was sad, really sad, man!"

"What happened? Who died?"

"Well, like I was saying, we had just walked away from the swings next to the big building where the swimming pool was. We heard all that screaming. People were running to the area we had just left. Eddie and I pushed our way through the crowd, wanting to see what happened. Then when Eddie and me made our way in, we saw it!"

"What? What did you see?"

"We saw a lady screaming her guts out, yelling and screaming! Man, we never saw anything like it before."

"Why was she screaming? What happened?"

"Well, someone from way up on the hill, by the road that runs up there to get out of the park, was fooling around and let a rock come down, a big rock, about the size of a basketball. Big, man!"

"The lady was crying and screaming because she saw a rock come down? I don't get it, Arthur. Maybe it's the beer getting to me."

"No, the rock came down hard and smacked her five-year-old kid right in the head. There was blood all over the place. You couldn't even tell who the kid was from all the blood and the way he looked. It was ugly man! I'm telling you, I never want to see anything like that again."

"Wow, really? Poor kid, man. Did you cry?"

"Me? Na, I didn't. But I'll say this, it was sad. I heard someone yelling my name and then the person yelled for Eddie."

"Why would they be yelling your name? Did you know them?"

"Yeah, I knew them. It was my mom. She was really scared. She thought it might be us who were smacked by the rock."

"I thought you said the kid was only five years old," Phillip asked, not understanding.

"He was, but you know how mothers are. They are always worried when there's no reason to be."

As I said this, I thought of my mother, how sad she was when I left the house awhile back. I thought of all the times she was there for me when I needed her most.

Once, when I was six years old, I lived on Spencer Street the west side of San Jose in a little house. The house was a one bedroom with a small living room and a big kitchen. My father liked bright colors, so the outside of the house was very bright. It looked like a cartoon house. The house was white with bright blue trim. The front porch was painted bright red and bright blue and yellow. Across the street were our friends the Rivas'. Gloria, the oldest girl, was my age. Her younger sister Blanca was a year younger than I was. They both went to Gardner Elementary School with me.

I was over their house playing when my brother Eddie came for me. "Arthur, Mom said to come home. Now. We're leaving. Hurry!"

"Where are we going?"

"I don't know. I think swimming. Mom got our things she always gets when we go swimming."

"OK, I'm coming." I turned and told the girls, "I'll see you Blanca and Gloria."

I ran across the street as they stood on their lawn. They appeared unhappy, wishing they could go swimming also. My father was at the back of his 1951 green Pontiac loading up the trunk.

I was running toward the house when Dad saw me. "Arturito," Dad called as I neared the house.

I stopped and ran toward him. "What, Dad?"

From inside the house my mother called. "Arthur, come here! Arthur!"

"Go. See what your mother wants," Dad instructed. As I started to walk away my father insisted, "Run!"

I ran into the house and saw my mother putting some of my things in a bag. "What, Mom?"

"There you are, Mijo! Come here," she said as she reached out for me. She pulled me close to her and said in very lovingly, "You are so cute! I love you." She gave me a big hug and then gave me the longest kiss. I didn't know what I did to deserve it; nevertheless, it felt good. As my mother held me close, I smelled her perfume. I loved Mother's fragrance. If she wanted to hold me all day and all night, I would let her. "Here, take this to the car. We are going to take you kids to a nice place today to have fun," she announced as she handed me a bag with all my clothes in it.

"OK, Mommy. Do you want me to take them to Dad?"

"Yes, Mijo. Then come back and help me with other things I have to take."

I was excited knowing we were going swimming. It was a very hot morning, and I knew as the day went along that it was going to get a lot hotter. I ran to the car and gave the bag to my father and ran back for more things. My father was whistling as he put the bag in the car and was moving other things around in the trunk. When my father whistled, it meant he was in a very good mood and would probably stay that way for the rest of the day.

As I came back out with another bag, my father's friend drove up to the front of the house. His car window was open, and he yelled out as his car came to a stop in front of the driveway. "¿Qué pasa, José? Almost ready?" He opened the door and stepped out of his car. I really didn't know Jorge very well. At times he would leave with my father and not come back for the rest of the day. Jorge's wife and his two young kids were in the car waiting. My mother came out to talk to his wife Ruby.

My father closed the trunk and turned toward Jorge. "Quebole (What's up), Jorge, ¿qué pasa?"

"I'm ready to go. How about you?" Jorge replied.

"Sí, I am ready," my father answered in Spanish.

"All right, let's get going before it gets too late," Jorge declared in Spanish. They always spoke only Spanish to each other.

We drove into the Santa Cruz mountains which were covered with redwood and pine trees. Some parts were dense with redwood trees. We arrived at the park where our parents took us at times to spend the day. The air smelled fresh and clean; the park had a lot of green grass. In some spots it was even cold because the trees were so thick that the sun couldn't shine through them.

We piled out of the car. I couldn't wait to jump in the water. The water came from a stream that ran along the side of the road and

into the park. It emptied into a large, deep lagoon.
As we were setting up our spot on the grass, I told Mom I needed to change into my swimming trunks, as did Eddie. My father told me to take my clothes off right there in front of everyone, but I wouldn't. It seemed as if he was joking, but I wasn't sure.
"Change right here because we are not going to take you to change somewhere else. Anyway, you don't need to hide; you are just a muchachito and don't have anything anyone wants to see," he stated.
I knew I was just a little boy; however, I wasn't going to show myself off to anyone! I didn't care how young I was. They had bathrooms at the park, but they had no doors on the stalls. I usually wore my trunks under my pants, but today I didn't have time to put them on at home.
My mother said, "Ay, Mijo, come here. I'll fix you up." She had a large blanket she was just going to spread out on the grass. She made a tent with it. I crawled into the makeshift tent. It seemed as if I were in a little tee pee. I quickly removed my pants and shorts, hoping no one peeked in or yanked the blanket from over me at that moment.
At this particular park the water was too deep for children. There was an 8-foot by 8-foot steel platform that was two and a half feet beneath the water. It had a chain around it, so kids couldn't step off very easily. As Eddie and I approached the platform, there were already six kids standing on it, yelling and splashing. Tita was too small to get in; even the platform was deep for her. She was content to sit and play around Mom. Mom would take her and wet her down whenever we went to places where the water was too deep.
Dad and his friend dove into the deep water without testing to see if it was cold first. Before I stepped onto the steel-sheet platform, I stood and observed my father and his friend dive into and swim in the water. Dad seemed as if he were going to drown because he wouldn't come up for the longest time.
"Arthur, Eddie," Mom called. "Be careful! Remember that it's deep! Don't go beyond the chain!"
Eddie and I looked at Mom, and Eddie answered, "We won't, Mom!"
I looked at Mom with her worried expression. She was always concerned about us, watching our every move from a distance to

make sure we were all right. My father would tell her to leave us alone, that we would be all right because we were boys, and that boys were made to be rough.

I sat on the bank, which was a concrete ledge. Sticking my feet in to see if it was cold, I tested the water, thinking it was going to be really cold on a hot day. It wasn't. Eddie touched the water with one hand and then jumped in and splashed me.

"Hey, Eddie, watch it!" I said, not wanting to get wet just yet. However, it felt refreshing.

"Arthur!" Mom called again. "Is it cold?"

I turned around and saw Mom looking at me smiling. It always made her happy to see us having a good time. I waved to her and nodded my head, indicating that it wasn't cold.

She motioned back at me with her hand, signaling for me to take a dive.

I signed to her that I was about ready to take my first dip and pushed myself over into the water. My feet touched the floor of the steel platform. The water was mildly warm. It reached the center of my chest.

Some of the kids who were on the platform were splashing water and playing roughly. There was a big kid next to me bullying the other kids. If he splashed water on me, I was going to push him into the chain and splash him back. I knew if he pushed me back again, Eddie would take care of him for me. Eddie was a very good, older brother. He was responsible at such a young age.

Out of nowhere a big thing hit my legs. I looked down and saw something at my feet. It was touching me and trying to lift my foot to tickle it. I didn't know what to make of it. Next I saw a big head with dark black hair coming out of the water. It was my father! He came out of the water with his eyes wide open, saying, "Hooo! ¿Qué pasa muchacho?"

"Dad, you scared me! I thought you were a big fish!" I said, knowing my father was playing. When my father went on outings with us, he was in a good mood and was fun to be with; however, we still had to be careful not to upset him.

"José! Want another beer?" Jorge asked, standing at the bank with a towel around his neck.

"¡Pues sí, hombre! (Of course, man!) We have to finish all the beer we brought before leaving, you know! That means we have to do a lot of drinking!"

Eddie and I played on the platform for awhile. In about an hour, Mom called us out to eat. Eddie and I stepped out of the water and ran to where she was standing. She already had our sandwiches made. Dad and Jorge were eating, drinking, and telling jokes. They were having a good time. My sister Tita was playing with Jorge's children.

When I was done eating, I asked if I could go back in the water. "You have to wait a little while, Arthur; or you will get cramps. We don't want that to happen! You might drown! What will we do without our little Arthur if that happens?"

"That won't happen," I said, trying to sound convincing.

"No, you have to wait a bit," she insisted. I saw Dad look my way. I knew I had better not say anything else. He didn't like us to argue with Mom or him.

In twenty minutes my father and Jorge ran to the water and dove in again. I asked Mom if enough time had gone by for me to re-enter the water. She gave me ten more minutes. In about ten minutes I jumped back in as Dad and Jorge stepped out to get more beer. Eddie was playing with Tita when I left.

There were six kids playing on the platform; then three more ran toward us and jumped in, splashing water all over. The small platform was quickly becoming overly crowded. Two more big boys ran toward the platform, yelling to see who could get in first. They dove in; my head went under water as I was knocked to the other side of the chain. Even though my body was on the other side of the chain, my feet were still on the platform. Three bigger boys' backs were facing toward me. They didn't notice where I was.

Suddenly one of the bigger kids crowded me even more. I let go of the chain briefly as I tried to get a better grip of it. My head went under water again, and at that second my body moved away from the platform.

I completely lost my hold of the chain and went under the water. I reached for another part of the chain with both hands and touched it with my fingertips but couldn't grasp it. I reached again as I felt myself move away and missed! I felt myself go back even more. My toes were still on the metal. I tried to move my feet to touch one of the other kids, so they would know I was sinking into the deep water. My body moved away even farther from the platform. I reached for the chain again, trying desperately to grab anything. My head was under water, and I knew I wasn't coming back up again. The platform was gone from under my feet.

I opened my eyes under the water; it was very clear. I could see the other kids' feet moving around on the platform. I felt myself drifting down fast. The noise of the kids on the platform was barely audible and muffled. I felt myself sinking deeper and deeper. The sounds of the other children were soon gone.

It sounded as if bubbles were passing beside me. I knew my life was over as I went farther down. I saw the top of the platform disappear, and I wanted to scream; but I didn't even try. Being underwater, I knew it was useless. I do not remember being out of breath or fighting for air.

As I continued to sink, I saw a small school of fish swim toward me. I also saw my short life pass before my eyes, including my mother leaving for work and hugging me. I had a nightmare; I woke up under the bed screaming. My mother pulled me out and told me everything was all right. I saw Eddie and Tita laughing. I saw my mother walk into the house with her new baby in her arms. I reached up, wanting to view the new baby.

I wanted Mom to hug and hold me right then! I wanted her to kiss me and never take her arms away from me.

Inside my heart and mind I was yelling as loud as I could, "Mom! Mommy! Mommy, help! Help, Mommy, please help me, Mommy!"

I was crying in my heart and scared to know I was going to die and would never be held by my precious mother again. I loved her so much! I never ever thought anything could take me away from her. "MOMMY, HELP!" I yelled again in my heart and mind.

I could barely see the surface of the pool. No one saw me go under, and I was certain I wouldn't be saved! I looked down and saw the floor of the lagoon. It appeared as if it were sandy, or it was a brownish dirt. I didn't know why I still wasn't distressed about not being able to breathe. I was only upset about dying and not ever seeing Mom again.

I turned my body and faced up to see the sun radiating down

into the water. I believed it would be the last light I was ever going to see.

As I was looking up at the surface of the pool, out of nowhere I saw someone dive into the water. I wished that whoever it was saw me or knew I was almost at the bottom of the lagoon. The individual who dove in had his eyes wide open, and his hair was flowing back in the water. He was looking straight down at me. He moved his arms in a swan motion, swimming straight down. As he approached me, he reached me, his arm came toward me. His hand grabbed my hair. He started to swim with one arm up, with me in tow by my hair. I knew at that instant I was being saved and wasn't going to die. I knew I was going to be in my mother's arms once again.

As we blasted to the surface, I was fighting for air. Jorge lifted me up and out of the water. The person who saved me was Dad. He pushed me up toward Jorge. Mom was standing next to Jorge, crying for her little boy. As I grabbed for Mom, I spit up water. I wasn't crying at that point because I was in shock, but I was glad to be alive. My mother held me tight and told me everything was going to be all right. "It's OK, Arthur, it's all right," she said as she comforted me, patting my back as she spoke "You're OK now. Everything is going to be all right, Mijo!"

Dad stepped out of the water and placed a towel around me. "Arturito, you need to be careful. From now on you have to stay in the middle of the platform!"

My father didn't have to worry about my falling in the deep lagoon again. I wasn't planning on going into the water for the rest of the day. All I wanted to do was stay close to Mom and not move from her side.

Chapter Eight

Burned

"Hey, Phillip, let's get going, man! This rest is long enough."

"Come on," I said as I stood. I wanted to get my mind off my mother and the sad expression she had when I left.

Phillip threw his head back and stretched out his arms. "I don't feel like going anywhere. We should stay here and watch the cars go by. Who knows, maybe some girls will pick us up and take us away!"

"Yeah, right! I could just see two older girls driving by this early in the morning and picking up two guys half drunk and taking them for a ride!" I laughed.

"Yeah, man, I saw on the news that some girls picked up a man and kidnapped him the other day!"

I started laughing at the thought. "Come on, let's go, man!"

Phillip stood. He put his empty bottles under the bench where he was sitting. I left mine there also. We were used to drinking beer. In the last year we had been drinking a lot in the neighborhood. When Fred paid me for mowing his lawn, Phillip, Ray, and I would go and stand at a store waiting for an older person to come by who was willing to purchase our cheap beer.

"You don't believe me, huh? It's true, man! I'm telling you. I didn't believe it either. I had to read it over again! Man, I wish I were that guy!"

I started to laugh. I could see Phillip in that situation and wanting to run when some crazy old lady was kidnapping him.

"Hey, what are you laughing about, Arthur? You still don't believe me? I'm going to look for that paper when I get home, just to show you!"

The light turned green on Alum Rock Avenue, and we started to cross. "Look for it? I thought you said you saw it on the news! Besides, man, I could just see you fighting off an old, ugly lady who looks like a gorilla, trying to get you in her car!" Visualizing Phillip fighting a lady who looked like a gorilla, I almost fell to the pavement laughing.

Phillip didn't get what was so funny. Once he was halfway across the street, he understood the picture I was giving him. He started to laugh, took large steps, almost fell to the ground, and dropped his bag of beer. "Man, that poor guy! It must have been a lady who looked like that to want to kidnap a guy."

Both of us were bent over staggering with laughter. "Watch out, 'King Kong'!" Phillip yelled.

"Hey, you said you wished it were you! I can just see you with, 'King Kong'!" I shouted, bending over laughing.

Once we were done laughing and we were no longer saying anything, Phillip said, "Hey, Arthur, we should stop again and have some more beer."

"Stop? We only walked across the street. Let's walk a little more. We'll be there in awhile."

Phillip was quiet for a little while as we walked a little faster. We made good time to McKee Road, about a quarter mile away.

As we were walking, making good time on King Road, I asked Phillip, "Hey, Phillip, did I tell you what happened to that guy who went by us on McKee Road?"

"Which guy? Oh, the one you were staring at as he went by. The way you were staring at him, I thought you knew him. You should have flagged him down, so he could give us a ride to the flea market."

"I know him and his friends, but I don't think I would ask him for a ride."

"Why not, Arthur?"

"Well, here's the story."

I then proceeded to share this experience with Phillip.

I was thirteen. I took the bus to the Jose Theater to meet some of my friends as I did almost every Sunday. It was early. Usually my friends would arrive around two o'clock; that day it was only 1:30.

I bought a ticket and entered the Jose. Walking in the door, I was struck by the aroma of the popcorn. There were a lot of kids lined up at the snack bar. The Jose Theater was kept really nice. The carpet was red and blue with gold swirls as the pattern. They would show three movies over and over again. We would go and spend the entire day there. Once in a while we would pay attention to the movie but not that often. We'd rather hang out with our friends and walk around looking for girls than watch a movie. Occasionally I would get in a fight at the Jose.

I saw some guys I knew standing in the lobby against the wall; they were not the friends I hung around with on regular basis. I greeted them as I went up the stairs to the balcony. The balcony by the stairs on the second floor was where my friends and I would usually hang out.

I stood against the wall and waited. It was dark, and it took a bit for my eyes to adjust. As I stood there, an usher shined his light at me. "Hey," he said. He was a young usher who liked to stop and talk to my friends and me when he was making his rounds. Some of the other ushers were a lot older; when they made their rounds, they would ask us not to talk. If we were too loud, they wanted us to take a seat. The ushers wore suits with a gold stripe running down the side of their pants.

"Hey, Dave, how are you? Have you seen the other guys?" He knew whom I meant when I asked for the other guys because they were the only ones I hung around with.

"No, I just got here. If I see them, I'll let them know you're up here."

"OK, thanks, man." I said as Dave started down the stairs.

I walked through the back aisle against the wall. There were a lot of guys and girls standing, talking, and smoking. I continued moving to the other side of the balcony. Standing against the wall on that side were a bunch of girls and guys who were watching me. No one said anything as I passed, but they took puffs of their cigarettes as they studied me. I had been in a fight with a guy from the other side of town, and I didn't know if these were his friends. I thought maybe they were from the way they looked at me. I was a little nervous; however, if one of them were to say something, I was ready to take the first swing. I went down the other flight of stairs and went through the lobby and up the first flight of stairs again. I stayed at the top of the stairs against the wall where I usually stood with my friends. I waited there for a half hour. Different people would stop and greet me. One of these persons was Frank.

"Hey, Art, how you doing?"

"All right, Frank. What's up, man?"

"Not much. Where's the rest of the batos (guys)?"

"I don't know. They should be here soon."

"Hey, be careful. I know the batos from the west side are looking for some action, and I think they looked this way and were talking about you. So be careful, ese (guy). If you're here alone, they might come over here."

"Why? What did you hear them say?"

"I just heard they want to fight someone from the east side. Because of what happened with you and Charlie the other week, I think it's you they want to fight."

"Well, if it is, I'm ready anytime, man."

"I'm just letting you know to be careful, Art."

As we were talking, Johnny stepped up to us. "Orale, bato, how you doing?" Johnny asked me.

Johnny was nineteen or twenty years old. He had short, black hair and was on the short side. He had a round face and a hard stare. His complexion was dark brown. Johnny was a stocky loco. He wore black, baggie pants and a black shirt buttoned to the top. He didn't come to the Jose often, only once in awhile and didn't know Frank, even though they were both from the west side.

"Hey, Johnny, how's it going? Hey, this is Frank, my friend."

Frank wasn't really a good friend. He hung around with the guys from the west side, but he was OK. I was introducing them, trying to impress Frank that I knew Johnny.

"Orale, Frank," he said, looking at Frank and extending his hand. "I'm Johnny, ese (guy)."

Frank knew who he was because he saw him around and heard about Johnny and his fighting reputation.

"Hey, ese (guy)," Frank greeted Johnny. He turned to me and said, "Art, I'm going to go look for my babe, man. See you around."

"OK, Frank, I'll be here. Take it easy."

Frank walked away.

"Hey, Art, I just want to let you to know that Charlie asked me to come and tell you that there is no more pleito (problems) between him and you. Everything is cool as far as he is concerned." Johnny said this as if I was supposed to be relieved. The last fight I had with Charlie, I heard I broke two of his ribs right there on the balcony steps. I also left him full of blood from hitting him on his nose. After that fight, as I walked home alone, eight of Charlie's friends jumped me, all of them throwing punches. Some connected, and some didn't. I gave them a good fight before going down.

I didn't believe Johnny anyway. "Hey, Johnny, tell Charlie that anytime he wants to fight again I'm always ready; and it doesn't matter if he's alone or with his friends. I don't care, man."

"Orale, Art, like I said, he don't want to fight you anymore, ese (guy). He wants to be friends with you now. Hey, ese, you got any feria (money)?"

"Any feria? Why?" I did have $4.00 that I received from cutting Fred's lawn.

"These batos (guys) outside want to take you on a trip, ese. They have some good stuff, ese," Johnny said, stretching out the word 'ese,' sounding as if it were a really good thing.

"Good stuff? What do you mean good stuff, Johnny?"

"Come on, ese, let's go outside. I'll show you what I mean."

I didn't know what Johnny was talking about, so I asked again, "What do you mean good stuff? Beer? Whiskey?"

"No, ese. Come on, let's go and see outside."

He started walking, and I followed. Johnny was so much older than I was that I felt intimidated.

As we were walking hurriedly down the stairs, he said without looking at me, knowing I was anxious to understand what he was talking about, "Mota, ese!" He meant marijuana.

I had never seen it, let alone tried it, because I was only thirteen. In those days it was a big thing, and the consequences were really bad if one was caught with marijuana. If you were caught selling it, it could get you twenty years! Nonetheless, I was curious to see what it was. I thought if I tried it then I would be able to tell all my friends. I also wanted to know how it felt.

"Where are your friends, Johnny?"

"Outside, ese, come on," Johnny said as he slowed down to wait for me, not wanting me to stop. We started walking through the lobby. "Hey ese, you have feria (money), right?" he asked again, making sure we were not going outside for nothing.

"How much does it cost?"

As we walked through the lobby, Johnny said, "Four dollars a joint, ese. You got it, right?"

"Yeah, I have $4.00."

"A joint, what is a joint?" I asked again, not sure what he meant.

"A frajo (cigarette), ese!" he answered, as if I were really dumb for not knowing.

We approached the front doors of the theater. Six of Charlie's friends were outside, not the ones who jumped me but other guys. All had their eyes fixed on me. I had a feeling they were all meeting at the Jose to get me for what I had done to their friend Charlie. Some of these guys wore Pendleton shirts, buttoned all the way to the top, and khaki pants. Some wore Frisco jeans. They saw I was with Johnny and knew better than to start anything when I was with him. As I stepped out the doors of the Jose Theater, I bumped one of them on purpose. The guy wasn't giving me enough room to walk by, so I was making room.

"Hey, man!" he blurted out. He didn't like being bumped.

Johnny turned around first, not believing a kid was telling him, "Hey, man."

I turned toward him and asked, "You talking to me, man?" I didn't like them, and they didn't like me. I knew they didn't want to mess with me as long as I was with Johnny, no matter how many guys were with them.

"Hey, Art, leave the babies alone," Johnny said, telling the guy, "Hey, chavalon (little kid), behave yourself; or I'll whip you myself!" He stepped in front of me, turned, and told me, "Come on, Art, we don't have time for these chavalones." Johnny grabbed me by my shoulder and turned me around to walk away.

As I was walking away, I turned to look at the guy with eyes that said, "Next time, man! Next time!"

We reached the sidewalk and jogged across the street to the parking lot. There was a lot of activity on Second Street with all the cars driving on the street. During those years people went to town to shop. In the evenings kids went to cruise.

Johnny waved to two guys in a 1948 black, lowered Plymouth. The two guys were Johnny's age. They had the doors of the car open as we approached. Each of them had a quart bottle of beer.

The guy on the driver side said, "Ese, Johnny, did you get one?"

"Simon, (Yeah), ese. I told you I would. This is Art," Johnny introduced me. "Art, this is Flaco (Skinny) and Sambo."

Sambo said, "Hey, Art, get in the back seat with Johnny, ese. How much money do you have?"

Sambo started up the car and backed out of the parking space. When he turned to look for approaching cars, I observed his eyes. They were as red as a mad dragon. They also looked like tiny slits. He started to drive forward very slowly. I knew from the way he appeared that he was really stoned. He was doing the driving even though it was Johnny's car.

As Sambo pulled the car out of the parking lot, Johnny spoke up and said, "He has $4.00, ese. He wants to buy one joint."

I didn't know what to say. I felt as if I were a little boy with those older guys.

As Sambo drove down the street very slowly, he reached in his shirt pocket and pulled out a homemade cigarette. He reached back over his shoulder and said, "Orale, Art, here you are, ese."

I looked at it and realized it was the first time I had ever seen drugs. I took it.

"That will be $4.00, ese."

I reached in my pocket and pulled out my four wrinkled bills. "Here you go, Sambo," I replied, as I put them in his hand.

Johnny said, "OK, Art, light it up, ese."

Johnny took out a lighter and flicked it so that I could light the joint. I didn't know I was going to smoke it with them; however, I didn't think it would be a good idea to say anything. I put the joint to my lips as Johnny flicked his lighter again. It lit. Just as I was going to take a good puff from it, Johnny took it out of my hand. He took three big tokes from it. I watched how he kept the smoke in his lungs and wouldn't let it out. Sambo had his hand over the seat, signaling Johnny to pass it to him. He kept it there for the longest time. Johnny didn't want to release it. Finally he gave the cigarette to Sambo.

I thought, "The way Sambo looks, he's not going to be able to drive pretty soon!"

In a bit Sambo handed it to Flaco. Flaco kept it for the longest time and also didn't want to release it.

I thought, "Hey, man, it's mine. I'm not even getting any."

"Orale, Flaco, pass it back, ese! It's almost gone!" Johnny insisted.

"Hold your horses, ese! I'll give it to you in a second." That was the only thing I heard Flaco say. He was a guy with few words. In another two tokes he handed it to Johnny again. I put my hand out to get it, but

Johnny raised his other hand and motioned for me to be patient. Finally he gave it to me. Just as I brought it up to my lips, Sambo told me to hurry. I took a toke, but Johnny took it from my hand and passed it to Sambo.

We were riding down Vine Street about fifteen blocks from the Jose Theater when Sambo saw a cop car down a side alley.

"Oh, no, ese! He saw us. I think he's going to come after us, ese. And man, we have this chavalon (child) with us. Man, ese, I have all these joints here."

Sambo stepped on the gas, and we moved rapidly down the street. As we were flying around the corner, I looked out the back window and saw the cop car spin out of the alley as if he were coming after us.

"Quick, Johnny and Flaco, here!" he said as he handed them two joints each. "Eat them! He's coming! Ese, Art, I'm going to stop when I turn the next corner. Jump out as fast as you can, ese. I don't want to get busted for turning on a chavalon [coward]!"

We made a quick turn at the next corner and stopped abruptly. The door flew open, and I jumped out of the car. I wasn't even out when Sambo stepped on the gas. The car accelerated away.

I took a few steps as fast as I could to the sidewalk and started walking normally. In the event the cop came by, it wouldn't look as if I was just let out of the car. In a second the cop car came flying by me. As it went by, the cop glanced at me. I looked at him. He kept going.

Here I was clear on the other side of town with no money and no ride. I had a long walk home. I couldn't even get back in the Jose Theater because I had no money left.

I walked three blocks and turned on South First Street. I saw the Plymouth parked with three cop cars behind it and decided to walk by them. The cops had Johnny in the back seat of a cop car. Sambo and Flaco were sitting on the curb with a cop standing over them while two cops searched Sambo's car. They had the quarts of beer on top of the car. I knew right then that when they dropped me off they had done me a favor.

Johnny looked out the car window and saw me. He smiled, nodding his head as if he were saying, "Orale, ese, I took care of you." Actually, they burned me for my money. They only let me off because they didn't want to get charged for contributing to the delinquency of a minor because they had beer in the car.

Chapter Nine

The Tire Shop

"That's too bad, Arthur. Maybe someday you can get your $4.00 back!" Phillip exclaimed, a little upset that I was burned.

"I don't want my $4.00 back. That's why I didn't want a ride from him. Maybe he would take our beer and try to sell us another joint!"

"No way, man, I won't buy anything from them, not after that story!"

"I know. Sometimes when you're with those older guys, they make you feel like you have to do it or you're lame!"

By the time we arrived at the flea market, Phillip was really drunk. He was having a difficult time walking straight. I was pretty bombed myself but not as bad as Phillip.

We found Tom's tire shop. "Hey, Tom!" Phillip yelled as we approached it. Tom was talking to customers when he heard Phillip yell. He turned and looked our way; then he turned back toward his customer.

We walked into the shop. The tire shop had used tires stacked all over the place. It was built with a wood frame and had tarps hanging all around it. When the shop was open for business, the tarps were pulled back so that people could enter. I wondered if they took their entire stock of tires home with them at night because someone could easily steal them. I concluded that this wasn't possible because there were so many tires.

Tom wouldn't look at us; he was trying to show some people a tire. He said to them, "Yeah, $5.00 each. That includes mounting."

"Can I bring my car in here?" the customer asked.

"Yeah, just drive your car in . . ."

"Hey, Tom, man! We came to visit you! How you doing?" Phillip asked in a loud voice.

Tom appeared embarrassed. He looked at Phillip with an expression that said, "Oh, man, he's drunk!" He then replied, "I'll be right with you, Phillip and Arthur."

Even though we were only a few feet from Tom, Phillip yelled, "All right, Tom! We have all day!" Phillip then flopped down on some old tires to rest.

Tom didn't say anything more to Phillip. He kept conversing with the people to whom he was trying to sell tires.

"Hey, Arthur, sit on these tires. Man, I'm tired! That was a long walk!"

"I'll be back in a few minutes. I'm going to check things out," I answered as I stooped down, so the people couldn't see me. I took a drink of my beer and handed the bottle to Phillip, for him to take a drink.

Phillip stared at it with a disgusting look as if he was sick of the beer. "No thanks. I'll wait a little bit. Hey, where you going?"

"Just to check things out. For a walk. Want to go?"

"A walk? Are you crazy? We just got here from a long walk!"

"Yeah, man. I want to see if there are any girls I know here," I said as I stood to leave.

"Girls? Hey, I'll go with you," Phillip said as he started to stand. He stopped and flopped back down. "Nah, I better not. I don't feel like talking to girls right now, man."

"All right. I'll be back, Phillip."

Just as I started to walk away, Phillip said, "Hey . . . man, I feel really sick!" He had an ugly expression on his face as if he were seeing the end of the world in front of him. All of a sudden he opened his mouth and shot out a stream of fluid, hitting a stack of tires.

I jumped back a few feet, not wanting any of it to splash on me and just in case he was going to do it again. He started to stand. As he was getting up, he reached for a stack of tires to help support his weight as he continued to vomit. The ugly vomit was splashing all over the place, and it really stunk badly!

Tom stopped talking and looked at Phillip. He said, "Oh God! Man! Look at the mess! Shoot! My dad is going to be mad!"

I laughed to myself and thought, "Man, I know no girls will want to talk to Phillip right now!"

When Phillip was done, he went behind some tires and fell asleep.

Tom went for a bucket of water. It took him about five minutes to return. When he did, he threw it on the mess Phillip had made. He went to where Phillip was sleeping and said, "Hey, Phillip! Phillip, wake up!"

Tom mumbled something very low and walked away. In a few minutes he returned with another bucket of water. Again he splashed it on the mess.

Tom looked at me as I stood there holding a bottle of beer. He glared at me as if I should be helping him clean up Phillip's mess. I wasn't about to help. I wasn't Phillip's mother, and it wasn't my shop.

"Hey, Arthur, my dad is supposed to come here in a little while. If he sees you guys here drunk, he's going to be really mad at me. I hope he don't catch you here."

"When is he supposed to get here?" I asked, planning to get Phillip out of the store before that happened. I didn't want to get Tom into any trouble. He was already having a difficult time with the mess.

"I'm not sure, in about an hour or so, man."

I looked to where Phillip was sleeping, then back at Tom, and said, "OK, I'll try to wake him and get him out of here."

Tom looked over at where Phillip was lying, feeling badly that he was kicking us out when we went to visit him. "Well, let him sleep for a little while; then you can go before my dad gets here."

"Hey Tom, you are all right, man! Thanks, because I really don't think I can wake him right now."

"Yeah, Phillip's not a bad guy. I just got mad that he threw up in here. Man, it smells bad!" Tom exclaimed as he walked away to get another bucket of water.

The customer went to get his car, in order for Tom to mount his tires. I took my beer and went for a walk. In a short while I wasn't feeling well myself and decided to return. I had drank enough beer.

Returning to the tire shop, I found Phillip was still asleep. I woke him and told him we had to leave. He was out of it and didn't want to go anywhere. "Hey, Phillip, we can't stay here, man. Tom's father is coming right now, and he don't want us here."

Phillip didn't look as if he was drunk anymore. However, he was still sick, moaning, groaning and rolling on the ground, saying that his stomach was all upset.

"Arthur, call my uncle Johnny, man. He'll come and pick us up. I can't walk home. I can't," he moaned, rolled over, and coiled up to go back to sleep.

"Phillip, wake up, man! Do you know his phone number?"

Phillip didn't answer. He was sound asleep again.

"Man, I know you can't be asleep that fast, Phillip. Hey, wake up!" I took Phillip by his shoulder and shook him. "Phillip! Phillip, wake up!"

Phillip opened his eyes and stared at me with an expression as if he were saying, "You, again!"

"What? Leave me alone, Arthur."

"Hey, do you know your Uncle Johnny's number?"

"No," he responded, closing his eyes as if he went back to sleep.

I raised my voice loud enough for him and everybody around us to hear me, "Man, guess I'll have to carry him all the way home!"

Without opening his eyes, he whispered, "It's in my wallet." He didn't say anything after that.

I removed his wallet and looked for Johnny's number. Phillip had a small phone book. The phone number wasn't hard to find.

"Hey, Tom!" I called.

Tom was right outside the shop removing a tire. "Yeah, what's up?" he answered as he stood.

"Hey, where is a phone booth? I need to call for a ride."

"Over there by the snack bar," Tom answered as he pointed to the small snack bar in the center of the flea market.

"OK, Tom. Be right back!" I called out as I walked away. I knew Tom was relieved to know I was calling for a ride to get Phillip out of his shop before his father arrived.

I dialed the number and Johnny answered.

"Hello?"

"Johnny, this is Art, Phillip's friend."

"Oh yeah, kid, how are you? Is everything all right?" he asked, knowing I had never before called him.

"Well, Phillip and I are at the flea market, and Phillip kinda drank too much. We need a ride home."

"Drank too much? It's only a little after 11 o'clock. Were you guys out all night? How did you get there?"

"No, we started drinking early and walked here. But Phillip can't walk back."

"Let me talk to my nephew, Art."

"He can't talk, Johnny; he's passed out."

"Passed out? Man, that kid! His mother told me he's been drinking a lot lately. Where did you guys get the beer?"

I really didn't want to say, but I knew Johnny was cool. Johnny was Phillip's uncle from his father's side and not from his mother's side. "Well, Manuel and his mother had a party last night; and they left all this beer . . ."

Johnny knew from the way I sounded that I also had too much to drink. "Hey, Johnny, if you can't give us a ride, that's OK, man. I think I can carry Phillip home," I said, knowing Johnny would never let me do that.

Johnny laughed. "OK, Art. Have my nephew out in front, and I'll leave right now and pick you guys up. Do you think you can do that?"

"Oh yeah, I can do anything, Johnny."

"OK, Art, be there," he said and hung up the telephone.

I was feeling worse from all the drinking as the minutes passed. I walked back to the tire shop. As I approached, I saw Tom's father scolding him in the back of the shop. I stepped in, and Tom's father turned to look at me.

Tom's father asked him, "Who is that?"

"He's my friend, Dad."

"The one who stunk up the place?" he asked Tom.

"Man," I thought. "Phillip sure made a mess that won't go away! If his father can still smell it, it must be really bad or he has a very good nose!"

"Hey, boy, whata you doing here? Why did you throw up in here? You knowa how bad its a stinks?" he asked as he started walking toward me.

I didn't reply. I stepped over a tire to where Phillip was. Tom's father had not seen Phillip up to this point.

"Hey, Phillip, wake up, man," I said, hoping it wasn't going to be difficult to get him going.

"Hey, boy, whatcha you doing? Another one?" He turned around and looked at Tom and yelled, "Tomas! Come here! Whatsa this? Why you not tell me about this one?"

Poor Tom. I knew it was trouble for him. "Yeah, Dad?" he answered as he looked at me. I knew Tom was aware I was trying to get Phillip out of his shop.

"They're leaving, Dad. They're leaving right now."

"Phillip, come on, man! Let's go!" I picked Phillip up and put his arm around my neck.

As we started walking out, Phillip asked, "What? What's going on?"

"Hey, man, we got to get out of here. Tom's dad is upset," I whispered, trying not to let Tom's dad hear me, even though I knew he could. I walked Phillip out the front of the shop to the walkway where all the foot traffic was passing.

Because of the amount of beer I drank, I felt stronger than usual.

As Phillip was hanging onto me with his arm around my neck, he asked, "Where we going? I can't walk home. Hey, did you call my uncle Johnny?"

"Yeah, I called him," I replied.

"What did he say?"

Just as Phillip said this, I thought it was really funny how Phillip came to my house to take me out for a good time. Here I was with Phillip, as sick as a dog and with Tom's father staring at us as if he wanted to kill us and his own son Tom! I visualized Phillip standing at my bedroom window with his beer as if he were a cat who caught a mouse.

People were staring at us, realizing we were drunk. I busted out laughing! I then tripped on my own feet, and we both fell to the ground.

Tom's father stood at the entrance of the tire shop totally annoyed with us. The people who were walking by couldn't take their eyes off us.

I stood up. Phillip didn't. I told Phillip I wasn't going to carry him. He might as well get up and walk. He looked at me for a second and then lay down on the pavement to go back to sleep.

"Hey, Phillip, come on, man. Your uncle is going to meet us in front by the creek!"

The creek that traveled through Alum Rock made it's way all the way down to the flea market.

"He said he was leaving his house when I talked to him. I think he should be out front now. Come on, man! You could go to sleep in his car." I took his arm to help him stand up to walk.

Phillip's uncle Johnny lived a mile from the flea market on Jackson Avenue. We waited ten minutes before he arrived.

Johnny pulled over to where we were sitting. I stood and said, "Wake up, Phillip! Your uncle is here."

Phillip opened his eyes and stood, almost falling over. I caught him before he went down and helped him sit in the back seat. He slumped over as soon as he was inside the car. I rode shotgun.

As we drove away, Johnny asked, "How long have you been here?"

"We were only here about an hour before I called you."

"When did you start drinking?"

At this point I felt really tired. I knew I had way too much to drink and knew I needed to go to sleep. I felt like throwing up right there and wanted to lie down and go to sleep.

"Around seven this morning."

I put my head back on the seat and closed my eyes. Everything started to spin. I sat up and opened my eyes. It stopped. I put my head back again and closed my eyes. The spinning was worse. I knew I was going to throw up! I opened my eyes again.

"Hey! You all right, Art? You going to get sick on me? Let me know if you are, so I can pull over. I don't want you to get sick in my car, guy!"

"Yeah, I think I'm going to get sick. You better pull over right now."

Johnny pulled over on King Road. As soon as he started to, I opened my door as fast as I could. The car had not come to a complete stop before I began vomiting.

"Gee, Art, look what you did to my car," Johnny cried out, disappointed in me.

I couldn't answer, even if I wanted to. I was too sick and felt as if I were going to die. I knew right there that I was never, ever going to drink again! Never!

"Hey, Art, don't go to sleep on me now. You're almost home."
I opened my eyes because I thought my father might be home. "Stop, Johnny! Don't take me home!" We were a half a block from my house. "Leave me off right here. I'll walk the rest of the way. I don't want my father to see me right now."
Johnny glanced at me and saw how bad I looked. He understood. He didn't want my father to think he had anything do with my getting drunk.
"All right, Art."
He pulled over into a driveway on the same side of the street where I lived. I opened the door and stepped out of the car. I closed the door and looked at Phillip lying on the back seat. He was knocked out. "I hope you can wake him up, Johnny."
Johnny looked in the back seat at Phillip and said, "Na, I'll let him sleep. I'll take him home with me, call his mother, and tell her he is with me. I don't want anything to happen to him. He has it hard enough as it is."
Johnny was cool. I had uncles like him too; but they lived in Wilmington and San Pedro, California.
"Johnny, thanks for coming and getting us. You're a lifesaver, man! I really appreciate it. Man, I don't know how I would have got Phillip home. He really had too much to drink!" I said, leaning on Johnny's car door with my arms folded on top of the window frame. I then rested my head on my folded arms, looking down at the ground.
"Well, kid, I think you had too much to drink too. I know, look at my car door!"
"Man, I'm sorry about that Johnny. I really am."
"Don't worry. I'll tell Phillip he was the one and make him clean it up."
I laughed a little even though I was still really sick to my stomach and also very tired.
"Hey, Art, you want to come to my house and sleep it off with Phillip? I'll bring you home later."
Johnny was such a good guy, and it was a good offer. However, I thought of my mother when I left the house, how sad she looked. I didn't want my father upset with her anymore than he was already. Lately my mother had been fighting back with him more. In the past

she would never say anything in return. This was no longer the case.

"No thanks, Johnny. I better go home. I'll crawl in through the back window and go to sleep in my room. If my father says anything, I'll just have to deal with it."

Johnny put the car in reverse and said, "OK, take care, kid. You and my nephew have to be more careful. One of these days you're going to get into some trouble and get sent to Juvey, and all of this won't be worth it."

I knew he was right from the way I felt at that moment. I wanted to fall right there on the sidewalk and curl up as Phillip had done at the flea market. "OK, Johnny, see you. Thanks."

Johnny backed his car out of the driveway and drove away. I looked toward my house and couldn't see my father's beige Cadillac from where I was standing. I knew he would be home, but I wished he wasn't. I wouldn't have to deal with him. I hoped he wasn't upset and waiting for me.

As I walked the next few steps, I thought of when we hopped the back fence. I thought I saw my father; Phillip did too. I hoped I was wrong.

I was now five houses away and could barely make out my father's car. With the next few steps I took, I confirmed his car was there. He was home. My stomach felt like dropping to the floor. I wished I had gone with Johnny; I wouldn't have to hear my father call me names.

"If he calls me names, I'm leaving and I don't care what happens," I thought.

A few months earlier my father had been really upset with me. When he told me he hated me, I yelled at him and left. "I'll do it again if he yells at me!" I thought.

I wasn't a little kid anymore. Many thoughts were running quickly through my mind as I approached my house.

Chapter Ten

Saturday Night

I was fourteen years old. My father was going out all the time. Even during the weekdays he would go with his friends to Ralph's Bar on Story Road. Most of the time he wouldn't return home until late at night. A year before this I saw my father with another woman, which shocked me. From then on I didn't blame my mother for anything she did.

My mother had also started going out on Saturday nights with Sarah and her sisters and Sarah's brother, Pete. I really did not know Pete well, but he would greet me when he saw me at Sarah's house or one of her sisters' houses. Gina was one of Sarah's sisters and had also become very good friends with my mother. Gina had a son about my age. Paul was tall and big; he had become my friend over the years.

On this particular Saturday night, Rebecca was also going out with my mother. Rebecca was a very pretty lady, younger than Mom.

The phone rang. Tita answered it. "Arthur, it's for you!" Tita yelled out. Tita and I had become close during those last few years, having the same group of friends or hanging out at the Lopez girls' house or the hamburger stand at the corner of King Road and Virginia Place. During this time Tita's best friend was Sandy Lopez; she was the youngest of the girls.

"Hello," I answered as I sat on the sofa.
"Hey, Art, this is Paul. What's up?"
"Not much here. What about you?" I asked. I knew Paul was calling to see what I was going to be doing that evening. He liked hanging out with our group of friends, especially since the Lopez girls were his cousins.

"Oh, nothing. What are you doing tonight?"

I knew Paul had something going on in order for him to call to see what my plans were.

"Me? No plans as of yet. Maybe Phillip, Bobby, and I are going to do something. Why? Do you know where any parties are?"

"Yeah, I do."

"Oh yeah, where?"

We did know how to drive; however, we were too young to have driver's licenses. Most of the time none of us had access to a car. We had to walk to the parties.

"Here, man!"

"There? You having a party? Is your mom letting you throw a party, Paul? Are you kidding?"

"No, but my mom, my aunt Sarah, your mom, and my uncle Pete are going out tonight. My mom said I could invite you over to be here with us."

"With us? Who else is going to be there?"

"The girls, who do you think?" When Paul said the girls, he meant his cousins, the Lopez girls.

"Hey, cool. Ask your mom if I can bring Bobby and Phillip."

I already knew the answer to this question, but I wanted to ask anyway. Even if Paul didn't ask if we could go over, we would have probably shown up at his house. We liked being with the girls when they went to their aunts' houses. They would always call us and let us know where they were.

"What do you think, Arthur? Of course they can come!"

"Cool, all right! I'll call them and let them know."

I hung up and called Phillip, telling him the good news. He was ready to do whatever I wanted. Phillip was free during the weekends because Manuel and his mother enjoyed going dancing.

"Phillip, call Bobby and let him know we're going to Paul's house."

"All right. How we going to get there?"

"Well, I could ask my mother; but she has her friend with her. So I think it'll be best for us to walk. It won't take us long to get there. Hey, where can we get some beer?"

"I think Manuel has a six pack in the refrigerator. I'll take it. He'll think he drank it. And if he says anything to me, I'll tell him I don't

know anything about it. He'll think Jerry took it." We both laughed.
"OK, Phillip, I'll go by your house about 7 o'clock and pick you up."

I hung up the telephone. Tita heard me talking and asked what was I going to do. "I'm going to Paul's house with Phillip and Bobby."

"I'm going too. I'm going with the girls later."

"I know you are," I answered.

"You want me to go and ask Mom to take you and Phillip? She will."

"Na, that's OK. We'll walk." Gina didn't live far away. She lived close to San Antonio and King Road.

I went to my bedroom. Eddie was getting ready to leave. "Where you going, Eddie?"

"Out."

"I know you're going out, but where?"

"I don't know, with Fernando and Richard."

I could hear Rebecca and my mother getting ready in the bathroom. They were talking and laughing. My mother was very pretty. Mom was 34 years old. When she was dressed to go out, she was even prettier. I wondered why my father would rather go with other women than my mother.

Rebecca had long, strawberry blonde hair. She was a short woman with a nice figure. Rebecca wore a short, tight, red, sparkling dress. She had rosy cheeks and bright red lipstick.

While Eddie and I were in our bedroom, I heard someone talking outside as they walked by our window. It was either Eddie's friends or mine. I heard someone knocking on the back screen door. Tita yelled out, "I'll get it!"

I could hear the person speaking. "Hi. Is Eddie home?"

"Yeah, I'll call him. Eddie!" she yelled. "Come in, Fernando. He's in his room."

Fernando came into the house, followed by his brother Richard. As Fernando entered our bedroom, he asked, "Eddie, ready? Let's go."

Fernando looked at me and said, "Hey, Arthur, what are you doing tonight, big shot?"

"I'm going out with my friends. Hey, do you know where any parties are?"

Fernando gave a little laugh and smiled with only one side of his face, as he did sometimes. He thought it was funny that a young kid wanted to know where the parties were going to be. I was thirteen at this time, and Fernando was seventeen. To him I was young.

"Parties? Let me think. Well, I heard there is going to be one on Sunset and another one on Delmas on the west side, on Delmas and Bird. And there's something going on at the Azteca Hall on 24th and San Antonio. That's all I heard so far. I know I'll hear about more of them later."

"OK, I'm ready!" Eddie exclaimed as he finished tying his shoes.

"OK, Arthur, take care of yourself. And don't get into any trouble! Need some money?" Fernando asked as he took out a couple of quarters.

"Na, I don't need any. Thanks." Quarters were OK when I was younger, but quarters just didn't do it for me anymore. "I'll see you later, Fernando."

My little nine-year-old brother was standing at the doorway of the bedroom. He saw me turn down two quarters and said, "I'll take them!"

"OK, little kid, here," Fernando said as he put them in Victor's hand.

Eddie picked up his light jacket and said, "See you, Arthur."

"OK, Eddie, see you tomorrow."

I knew I wouldn't see him until the next day. During this time we were not worried about our father coming home and not finding us there. More than likely he wouldn't return himself.

Richard, Fernando, and Eddie stepped out of the bedroom. Eddie told my mother, "Bye, Mom."

"OK, Mijo, be careful. Where are you going anyway?" she asked as she stepped out of the bathroom and into the hallway to speak to Eddie.

"I don't know, Mom. I'll be back later," Eddie said as he kissed her.

"OK, Mijo. What time will you be back?"

"Later, Mom. I'm not sure."

"OK. Try to be back before your father gets here."

We all knew that wouldn't be until the next day. When we returned and his car was in the driveway, we would sneak into our bedroom window.

Eddie left. I thought it would be a good idea to take a shower before I left, but I had to wait until my mother and Rebecca were out of the bathroom. I lay on my bed and waited and thought about what I was going to do that night. In a while I heard someone outside of the house by my bedroom window. I thought Eddie forgot something. Someone knocked on the back screen door. Tita called out again, "I'll get it!"

"Hi, Dan. Do you want Arthur?" Dan was a year younger than I. When I was younger I hung around a lot with him in our neighborhood. He is Fernando's little brother.

I also heard a man's voice. "We were looking for Fernando and Richard. Are they here?"

"No. They left with my brother Eddie."

"Do you know where they went?" the man's voice asked.

"No, but my brother Arthur might. Do you want me to call him?"

"Yeah, would you?"

If it was only Dan at the door, I knew Tita would have let him enter. However, because it was a man, she thought it wouldn't be a good idea. "Arthur! Someone wants you at the door!" Tita called.

I left my bed and went to the back door. My mother and Rebecca were talking and laughing in the bathroom. Just as I stepped in front of the bathroom door, Mom went to her bedroom where she had all of her makeup. Rebecca stayed in the bathroom, spraying her hair with hairspray.

As I stepped to the door, I saw Dan and his uncle. Dan's uncle Sam was his father's youngest brother. He looked just like his father but much younger. He was just a few years older than Eddie and Fernando.

"Hey, what's up?" I asked as I opened the screen and stepped out on our small porch.

"Hi, Arthur. Where did Fernando and Richard go?" Sam asked, trying to look in the house as he spoke. I didn't really know Sam. I had only seen him at Fernando and Richard's house once or twice.

Just as I was going to answer, Rebecca darted out of the bathroom and walked hurriedly through the washroom, where the back door was located, and then through the kitchen.

Sam saw Rebecca and thought she really looked nice in her short, tight, red dress. He commented, "Wow, baby! Mamma, come here!"

As Rebecca dashed through the kitchen, she turned her head and glanced our way, but kept moving out of sight. Sam turned to me and asked, "Who is she, Arthur?"

I was embarrassed because she heard Sam. I thought, "What if she goes and tells Mom, and Mom comes to find out what was said? What if Sam tells my mother something like that?"

I had an ugly feeling something bad was going to happen. I worried about what to do if he said something to Mom. I knew I couldn't let him get away with it and hated for things not to go well. He had a man's body, and I had a kid's body. I was no match for him; however, if he said anything, I would have to do my best to defend Mom.

He looked at me because I didn't answer and asked, "Well, who is that babe, Arthur?"

"Hey, Sam, you better leave."

I looked at Dan. He looked embarrassed because he had been a friend of the family for as long as he could remember.

"Leave? No way, man! Not with that babe in there! Let's go into your bedroom, Arthur."

Sam reached for the screen door handle. Just as he did, I leaned on the screen. He couldn't open it.

"Move, Arthur. Let's go in!" Sam requested again as he pulled on the door, trying to move me with it.

"Hey, Sam, you better leave," I tried to say in a nice way, not wanting to start anything with an older guy, or should I say an older man? I didn't want to start a fight just because he thought Rebecca looked nice. But if he thought my mother looked nice, and said something to her, that was a different story. I would have to take a beating!

"Come on, Arthur, move! Let's go in."

I knew it wouldn't look good if I took a man in the house. I could just see the look on my mother's face if he went into the house and into my bedroom. She would be really upset with me, and I would really receive a scolding if I let him in. Besides, I couldn't imagine what my father would do if he found out I let a man in the house with my mother there. I would be killed!

"You have to go, Sam! Right now!"

Sam saw the expression on my face and realized he had better leave. I felt he knew that I knew what he was thinking.

"OK. All right, kid! Don't get excited!" He turned and looked at Dan and said, "Come on, let's go look for them." They walked away. Dan turned as they stepped away from the porch as if he were saying, "Hey, Arthur, I'm sorry."

From the time he made the comment to Rebecca to the time he left, Rebecca went to find my mother. She told Mother what Sam had said to her. My mother wanted to know who said it and where he was. Rebecca told Mother he was with me at the back door.

My mother stormed out of her bedroom. I was just opening the door to re-enter the house when I saw Mom. Her face was as red as a tomato. "Arthur! Who is here?"

"No one, Mom. Why?" I answered as I opened the screen wider.

My mother stepped outside to examine the back yard. "Rebecca said there was a man here. Who was he?" she asked angrily.

"Oh, that was Sam, Fernando's uncle. He was looking for Fernando and Richard. I told him they went with Eddie."

"I don't want him over here anymore. If he comes back, you come and tell me right away! Do you understand? I'm calling Judy and telling her!" Judy was Fernando's mother.

Later that evening I picked up Phillip, and we walked to Paul's house. Bobby said he would meet us there later.

I knocked on the front door and Paul answered. "Hey, Paul! How's it going, man?"

"OK, come in. Come in my room." He held the screen door open for Phillip and me. His sister May was in the kitchen doing something. May was four years younger than I. His little sister Carol was two years younger than May. Carol was watching TV.

"Hi, little girl," I greeted Carol.

"Hi," she answered.

I saw May in the kitchen and greeted her. "Hi, May. What are you doing in there?"

"Hi. I'm getting something ready for later for the girls," she responded as she stopped and smiled.

"Hi, May," Phillip greeted also.

Just as we were going to step into the bedroom, Gina came out of her room. She heard our voices. "Hi, boys. How are you?"

"Oh, hi, Gina, I'm fine," I answered and let Phillip speak for himself.

"Hi, Gina. I'm OK, too."

I asked, "You're going out tonight with my mom?"

"Yes, if they get here. By the time they all get here, I don't know if we're going. They were supposed to be here fifteen minutes ago," Gina complained.

"I know they should be getting here soon because my mom went to pick up Sarah and she's at her house right now. Well, I don't know about now, but she was there when we left Phillip's house."

Gina replied, "Yeah. They called and said they were on their way. So they should be here anytime, Mijo."

We went into Paul's bedroom. I sat on his bed. Phillip sat on a small chair, and Paul sat on the floor. We talked about what was happening that night. Phillip told Paul he brought the beer and hid it outside before entering. We asked Paul if he could get anymore beer for us; he didn't think he could. We decided we would drink it out of straws because we thought it would make us get high. I told them about the parties Fernando had told me were taking place that night. Paul said we should walk to the Azteca Hall because it was less than a mile from where we were. Phillip felt we should just spend the evening there, with all the girls.

As we continued to speak, we talked about other things. In a little while I heard a lot of voices coming from the front door. I heard Sarah's laugh and knew they had arrived. From where I was sitting, I could see the living room and the front door. The first one in the door was Sarah; she was talking to the others.

Sarah was a really fun person. I always enjoyed going to her house, sitting with everyone else around her kitchen table, and listening to her tell us about things she did when she was young and growing up. Her stories were like mine but they go way back. She could have written a book. As she spoke, she would take a puff from her cigarette, pucker up her lips, and blow the smoke upward. She was the kind of person anyone could pour their heart out to. She was always sympathetic. Maybe that was why my mother liked her so much.

"I don't think you would be able to," she said to whomever she was speaking as she gave a big laugh, tilting her head back, showing her big, white teeth. I couldn't hear the rest of her sentence.

Rebecca followed her in the house, and then I saw Mom stepping through the threshold holding hands with Pete. That was the first time I knew something was up with those two. My father came to mind; I wondered how he would react to this. In fact, I thought that if he knew, he would kill Mom and Pete! I was shocked but at the same time I saw how happy my mother appeared. She was smiling and it seemed as if her face shined. My family was really doomed and there was nothing anyone could do about it. My heart hurt but at the same time I loved to see mom happy. It was a weird feeling. It hurt inside because I knew it was wrong but at the same time I was sympathetic. I could not imagine my father finding out. I wondered how many other families went through this. I had a feeling life was going to be coming to a big change.

My mother did not see me from where she had entered the house. She went into the living room with the group of friends.

Phillip saw me looking out at the people who were entering and asked, "Are they here?"

"Yeah, they are," I answered.

Phillip moved his head over to see who had arrived. By the time he looked in the living room, they all had moved into the kitchen.

I knew my mother was very lonely those last few years because my father left her alone so much and even went out with other women.

During this time I was very close to Mom. She had been my only outlet during those turbulent, adolescent years. If Mom went out dancing with her friends, I understood. As far as Pete was concerned, I had these mixed feelings. I really did not know how to feel about it.

"Oh, Millie," I heard Gina say, "Arthur is here."

"He is? He's here? I just left him at home. How could he get here so fast?"

My mother came to the bedroom and looked at me, "Hi, Arthur. How did you get here so fast, Mijo?"

"I don't know, Mom. Phillip and I walked. Where are you going dancing, Mom?"

"I don't know yet. Pete said he is taking all of us to a club that has nice music. I'm not really sure." Pete was a married man with small children.

As the months followed, Mom kept a lot of company with Sarah and her family. It was mostly the same group who went out together.

Chapter Eleven

That Dreadful Day

As I walked down the sidewalk, I slowed down one house before my home. I hoped no one was looking out the window and wondered where my father was in the house. I also wondered what my mother was doing. I knew she had gone out the night before with her friends.

I walked along the side of the house, still feeling very sick and wanting to stop in the bushes and throw up again. I tried hard to control myself because I hated the feeling that went along with vomiting. I felt like dying. I would rather die than continue vomiting and didn't want to get sick when I went into the house. My father wouldn't feel sorry for me one bit; he would just add to my agony.

I was behind our garage. Tita's bedroom window was in front of me. This was the room my mother had been using to sleep. I went over to the side of it, not wanting to be seen, and put my ear on the wall to determine if there was any activity in the house. I did hear someone speaking; however, I couldn't really make out what was being said. It sounded as if the voice was Tita's, but I wasn't sure. I do know that I couldn't hear a man's voice. I moved my head over a bit to peek inside and saw Tita lying on her bed, writing on a tablet with a small transistor radio next to her.

I waited a few minutes, hoping to see my mother. She would tell me if my father had asked for me. She would also tell me if there was anything I should know. There was no sign of her. I didn't want Tita to see me; she might say something too loudly and give me away to the others. I moved away from the window.

I went around the back of the house to the back door and peeked in to see if anyone was present. The house appeared quiet. I didn't want to take any chances by entering from this area; therefore, I left the back door and went to my bedroom window. I had to enter the house the same way I left, through the window.

I reached up and opened it, expecting to hear Eddie's voice telling me how dumb I was for taking a chance. I really didn't want to hear it. All I wanted was to lie on my bed and go to sleep.

Eddie wasn't in the bedroom. I crawled inside. As I was moving over the ledge of the window, I saw my bed. It felt as if my bed were calling me, saying, "Art, come, lie down on me. Rest your body from your long, hard morning!" My bed looked so inviting; I couldn't wait to take the offer it called out to me. Without removing any of my clothes, I flopped down on my bed.

As soon as I closed my eyes, the room started spinning as it did in Johnny's car. "Oh, no," I thought. "I hope I don't get sick! I really hope I don't!" I opened my eyes and said to myself, "I'm OK. I'm not going to get sick! I'm not going to get sick! I'm not!"

I climbed out of bed and stepped to the door. I didn't hear any noise in the house. I knew I would be sicker if I didn't brush my teeth after having been sick; therefore, I went into the bathroom and closed the door slowly and quietly in order to brush my teeth.

Once I brushed my teeth, I felt a little better. I went back to my bedroom. After shutting the door, I flopped on my bed again. I hoped I wouldn't have to brush my teeth again. My eyes closed.

My thoughts went back to my mother, thinking of her sad expression when I left that morning. I also thought of all the times she put up with my father through the years. There were many occasions my father would yell at her and call her names. During the past few months, it had escalated to the point that it seemed as if he was going to hit her, however, he never did.

I had an odd, strong fear and respect for my father. When he was manhandling my mother, but not hitting her, there was only so much I could do. I couldn't grab his arms to stop him. All I could really do was step in between them and beg him to stop. He would yell at Eddie, Tita, Victor, and me as we all tried to hold him back with our bodies. If we were in our bedrooms during the fighting and it sounded as if it was going to get violent, all of us would charge out of our bedrooms and try to stop them.

"Millie, what is wrong with you?" my father would demand. "Estupida! Let me see!"

He would grab my mother, pulling her by whatever she was wearing, almost ripping off her clothes. At times he would rip her garments. We kids would gather around, yelling, "No, Dad! No! Stop! Please don't hit Mom, please!"

At times I would try to grab my father's hand, never roughly, but mildly, trying to persuade him to let go of her. He never hit her, but he did call her many names and acted as if he was going to beat her. I hated it!

My father and mother didn't speak very much to each other anymore. We, as their children, really didn't know why, nor did we know what the fighting was about.

As I lay on my bed, my thoughts started to fade into a deep sleep. I drifted far away.

"What in the heck is going on?" was my first thought. I lay on my bed, waking from a deep sleep. Noise! A lot of noise! "What is going on? Is this a dream?" I thought. "Where am I?"

I had not opened my eyes yet, wondered if it was morning, and asked myself if I had to go to school. Was Dad fighting with Mom again? All these questions were running through my mind.

"Crying? Who is crying?" My eyes opened fast as I recognized the wailing of young children. I started to sit up on my bed, but the headache was almost unbearable. It felt as if my brain was loose in my skull. If I moved my head slightly one way or the other, my brain would surely hit the other side of my skull! It hurt as if someone kept hitting me with a hammer! I went back down on my mattress.

"AY, NO! MILLIE!" I heard Dad cry out. I didn't know what in the heck was happening. The wailing of young children continued. I held my head with both hands and sat up again, looking around the bedroom to see if Eddie had returned. When Mom and Dad were fighting, Eddie and I would usually come to the bedroom and ride out the fight there, unless it seemed as if Dad was going to hit Mom. We would then run out and try to prevent it.

I heard my father yelling or speaking very loudly in Spanish, but I couldn't make out most of what he was saying. The children I heard were not speaking as they wailed, just sobbing very loud as if someone had died.

"Something must have happened pretty bad. Maybe the unthinkable happened and Dad hit Mom!" I thought. If this happened, I knew I would have been really upset with myself for not being there for my mother.

I stood up next to the bed, not knowing how long I had been asleep. I was in a very deep sleep; and, if it wasn't for all the crying and yelling, I would have slept all day. I started to fall over from dizziness and also the bad headache. I grabbed onto the headboard to hold myself up until I had my bearings.

"Millie, por que (why)? Millie! Ay, Millie! Mi amor Millie, por que (why, my love)? Ay Millie! Mi amor! Millie!" Dad cried. Now I knew something had happened. My father's cry wasn't one of anger but of anguish.

I listened for my mother to respond but heard nothing. Starting out of my bedroom as fast as I could, hanging onto the bed and wall as I left, I had to find out what all the commotion was about, wishing it were nothing major. As I stepped into the hallway, I heard Tita and Victor sobbing hysterically.

"Millie! Millie!" Dad yelled, running around the living room with one sandal in his hand. "Ay, ay, ay!" he kept repeating as he moved aimlessly, looking for his other shoe. I didn't move from where I stood. I was startled, never seeing my father act like this. As I tried to figure out what the tragedy was about, I stepped over to have a better view of my father running around the living room.

"Millie! Why, mi Millie? Chulita, por que? You know I love you, Millie! Te quiero mucho (I care for you a lot)!

I looked around the living room, thinking maybe I was missing something; or maybe I was still in a deep sleep and having a nightmare. Eddie, Tita, and Victor were in Tita's bedroom crying. I turned from where I was standing to observe them, wanting to see what was happening in the bedroom.

Mom was lying on the floor in the center of the bedroom. She appeared as if she just fell in this spot. Victor and Tita were sobbing, smothered up against her body. A picture of her came to my mind, how she looked when I left her that morning. "Oh, how sad she looked; she must have been sick then," I thought.

I stepped into the bedroom. Tita and Victor kept sobbing without stopping. Eddie had his hands over his eyes and continued crying quietly. He kept rubbing the tears away from his face. I knew when I saw Eddie crying that it was something very serious. "Eddie, what's wrong? Eddie?" I yelled, wanting desperately to know what was happening. Eddie didn't respond.

Everyone was crying. My father was still running around wildly, talking to himself. Mom lay on the floor as if she were in a deep sleep.

"Millie, don't die! Don't die, Millie! Por favor (Please)! No te vayas (Don't leave)!

Dad picked up the telephone and started to bang on it after he dialed "O" for an operator. "Hello! Hello! Contestame (Answer me)!" he yelled.

I stared at Mom, wondering what Dad meant when he said for her not to die and not to leave. Her eyes were in a daze, her body still not moving.

As I stepped toward her, Dad was still crying out about how much he loved her.

Once I was next to her, she opened her eyes. Her eyes looked past me; she said to Eddie in a whisper, "Eddie, come here, Mijo. Come here."

Eddie didn't move from were he was standing. He was still wiping his face in shock.

"What happened, Mom? What is it?" I asked, not understanding the situation.

"My Arturito. I want to hold you, but I can't."

"Mom, please tell me what happened?" I questioned.

Tita and Victor were still crying.

I bent down and patted her forehead, brushing back her hair. She closed her eyes as I did this. It seemed as she couldn't move any part of her body. Her fragrance was the same as it always was, and I loved it.

"Arturito, I love you, Mijo. Always remember that," she said softy.

"I know you do, Mom. What happened, Mom? What happened to you?"

"Millie! Millie!" Dad cried as he pulled the long cord to the telephone to the doorway. "Millie, te quiero (I care for you)! OK? OK, MILLIE?" he asked, waiting for a reply from Mom.

Mom moved her eyes up toward him and then back to me. "Arturito, Mijo. I love you," she whispered.

"I know, Mom. I know!" I said as I lifted her a bit and hugged her. Whatever it was, I knew right then that I should have never gone with Phillip that morning. There was something wrong with Mom, and I should have been smart enough to stay with her.

"Hello! Come! Hurry! Come! My wife took a bottle of pills! She is dying! She is bad! Hurry!" Dad yelled into the telephone.

"Oh, Mom! Why, Mom? You're not going to die are you, Mom?" I asked as I started to cry along with my brothers and sister.

I looked toward the nightstand and saw an open empty prescription bottle on the floor. I knew that was what she took.

"Ay, Mijo. I'm sorry. You do know I love you. I do; I really do. I do very much, Mijo. Take care of my babies, Arturito."

I started crying even more. I didn't want to lose my dear mother. I couldn't imagine my mother leaving us and never coming back. I was lonely for her when she was away from the house for a few hours, let alone leaving us forever. Eddie, Tita, Victor, and I loved her as much as any child would love their mother.

Dad put the telephone down again and ran to the doorway of the bedroom where we were. "Millie, they want to know how you feel."

Mom didn't say anything. I looked at her also, wanting to know what she was going to say. She looked at Dad with an expression as if she didn't know.

"My children," she said as if she was going deeper into a daze.

Dad went into the bedroom and gave Mom a kiss on the forehead.

He ran back to the telephone. "Ay, carambas!" (An expression of being overwhelmed) he exclaimed as he replied in his broken English, "My wife does not know! Hurry, please!" He listened for a second and slammed the receiver down hard. Dad continued running around looking for his other sandal.

"Mom, Mom, why Mom? Don't leave us, Mom! Mother! Please don't leave us!" I cried.

At this point Eddie was holding Mom's hand. Eddie was still quietly crying. He was the oldest and tried to hold in his strong emotions. He had always been this way. When we were beaten by our father, sometimes he wouldn't cry or make a sound. This would upset Dad even more.

"Millie!" Dad cried out as he came into the room.

I looked at Mom. She was getting paler by the minute. She looked as if she wanted to go to sleep.

"MILLIE, they said not to let you go to sleep! Wake up, Millie! Wake up!"

"Mom! Mom!" I cried.

"Arthur, my baby. Be good. Be good, Mijo!"

"Ay, no! No! No, Millie! Mi amor! I am not going to Mexico! I will not leave you, mi amor!" my father cried. His place of work, American Can Company, was closing in just a few months. He had been saying he was going back to Mexico to live. Now with this tragedy, within these few seconds, he was changing all of his plans.

As I wept, I thought that he should have never told Mom he was leaving her. I wanted to tell him that he should have thought about all of this during the past few years when he was leaving her by herself. He should have treated Mom much better. She was a good mother and a good wife to Dad. She had always waited for him to cool down from his tantrums before saying anything in her defense. In the past she had waited for Dad when he went out on the weekends with his friends. From what I could see, she was never upset with him for leaving her alone for so long. She was always there for us, even though she had to contend with a domineering husband.

I could hear sirens racing toward us. It sounded as if there were many of them approaching from King Road down Virginia Place.

I looked at Mom again. She appeared as if she was going to close her eyes and never awake. I held her tight as if I would never be able to hold her ever again, not believing this was happening. I prayed I would wake up from the most terrible nightmare of my entire life. "Mom, don't go to sleep. Mom, stay with us, please!"

Eddie started speaking as he cried. "Mom, what happened? What is wrong? Mom, please don't let this be true. Please, Mom!"

The emergency vehicles came to a halt in front of our house. I heard Dad open the front screen door. He ran out to meet the police and whoever else had arrived. In a few seconds I heard Dad talking as they all came into the house. "Come in, hurry, this way, hurry!"

Mom looked as if she was going to go to sleep. Her eyelids were almost shut. She appeared as white as a sheet but tried to open her eyes wider and tried to move her lips, attempting to say something. She seemed as if she was fading fast.

"What, Mom? What?" I asked as I sniffled from crying so much. "What, Mom?" I questioned again as I brought my ear down to her lips.

"I love you, Mijo. I love you."

"Oh, Mom! Mom!"

It seemed as if an army was entering the house. As the police entered the bedroom, I turned to look at them. They were dressed in their leathers as if they were on motorcycles. The first police officer who stood behind me had a sad expression, observing four young children smothering their mother, asking her not to die.

"Kids, we need for you to go into the living room. We need to help your mother." He picked up Victor by his hips and passed him to the person behind him. Victor was screaming and kicking, not wanting to leave Mom's presence. Eddie and I stood and moved back and out of the room. Victor was handed back to a third person who walked him to the living room. It was hard to control Victor who was really going wild, not wanting to be touched by anyone at this moment.

The officer asked Tita again if she would get up and go into the living room. "Honey, you have to let us take care of your mother," he said gently as he helped her, holding her shoulders. We were all sobbing emotionally, unable to stop, knowing there could never be another sad day such as this.

We all stood on the opposite side of the living room, facing the bedroom where Mother was lying. It seemed as if there were a hundred people in the house.

The police were asked to move and make room for the ambulance attendants who entered with their stretcher. One cop who came out of the bedroom looked at us with empathy. My father was kneeling down with us, holding Victor, calming him.

We were trying to get a glimpse of Mom in the bedroom as they were attempting to help her. From where I was standing, I could see them pick her up and put her on the stretcher. All of the emergency personnel stated moving out of the bedroom. The stretcher was being wheeled to the ambulance. Mom looked so white; she didn't look like herself. "My poor mom," I thought.

Her still body bounced on the stretcher as they rushed her quickly through the living room and out the front door. Everyone followed, including us kids and dad.

Out on the street there were three police cars and an ambulance.

I couldn't see any motorcycles. The street was crowded with what looked like every neighbor from two blocks away. It seemed as if there were 500 people in a big circle surrounding our home. They didn't say anything. They just stood there and watched with the saddest expressions on their faces. They had no idea what had just happened in our family.

All of us followed Mom. The men who were pushing and pulling Mom on the stretcher stopped. One of the men jumped into the ambulance to make room for the stretcher. I was standing fifteen feet from Mom with Eddie, Tita, and Victor. Dad was talking to a police officer. Dad seemed as if he was trying to explain what happened. He told them that when he stepped out of his bedroom he saw Mom lying on the floor, not moving. Dad reached up with both hands and pulled his hair back, tilting his head back and up, staring at the blue sky for a few seconds.

I was watching Mom. She held her hand up about five inches. She was trying to move her eyes to look at me. I knew she was calling me. I ran to her side before they put her into the ambulance. She moved her lips to say something.

"What, Mom? What?" I held her hand and squeezed it. Her dry lips moved again, but it seemed as if nothing came out of them. I moved my ear down by her lips.

"Say it again, Mom. Say it again."

I could barely make out the words. She almost didn't have any breath left. "Take care of my babies, Mijo. Take care . . ." She closed her eyes.

"OK, Son, move so we can take her to the hospital," one of the ambulance men said kindly.

"Mom! Mom!" I called as they moved her away and into the ambulance. I thought it was going to be the last time I would see her alive.

Dad ran toward the house, stopped, and ran back. He didn't know what he was going to do. He opened the door of the ambulance and said he was going to follow them. He looked back at us, closed the door of the ambulance and said he would drive himself. The ambulance fled away.

We stood and watched them all back out of our long, dead-end street.

Chapter Twelve

The Hospital

Dad took us in the house and told us he would call from the hospital at his first opportunity. We wanted to go with him; however, he said it wouldn't be a good idea at that moment.

"Everything is going to be all right. I will call you right way, ninos (kids). Your mother will be all right," Dad assured, trying to be positive.

"Dad, I'm going," I insisted.

"No, Arturo, you stay with your hermanos y hermana (brothers and sister). I will call you, I said!" Dad knew my character and knew I always wanted to do things my way.

I didn't say anything in reply. It wouldn't have made a difference. When Dad used that tone, I knew he wasn't going to change his mind. He picked up his cigarettes and keys and walked up to us to embrace us all individually. He told us all to be brave and headed out the door. This was odd for him to show kindness to us in this way, then again it wasn't just any day.

We all sat in the living room. It was very quiet. Just a few minutes before this, our house was swarming with people; and there was so much commotion taking place. Now there was no one, and everything was still and quiet.

Eddie stood and picked up the receiver of the telephone. He looked up Uncle Ben's phone number in our phone book and dialed his number. We sat and watched.

"Hello, is Uncle Ben home?" Uncle Ben was my mother's brother. Mom was the oldest of her family of eight, followed by Aunt Annabel and then Uncle Ben.

"Hi, Uncle Ben," Eddie said as he sniffed and tried to hold back his tears.

Uncle Ben was asking what was wrong. Eddie couldn't talk for a few seconds. "Uncle Ben, they just took my mother to the hospital."

After a long pause Eddie continued, "She just like fainted and couldn't move." He started to cry a little. All of us kids started to cry again.

He didn't want to tell Uncle Ben what really happened. In a few seconds Eddie stopped crying, listened, and then acknowledged, "OK, Uncle Ben. OK. OK." Eddie hung up the telephone.

"What did he say, Eddie," Tita asked.

"He said everybody is coming over right now. He said he loves us."

I stood. I didn't want to wait for reports about my mother's condition. I was going to the hospital even though Dad didn't want me to go. I wasn't going to let Dad keep me from Mom.

"I'm going to the hospital," I said as I started to walk toward the door.

Eddie stood up and replied, "Arthur, Dad said you have to stay. If you go, he's not going to like it very much."

"I don't care. I'm going. I want to be there with Mom."

I didn't want to leave Tita and Victor, but I couldn't stay there and wait. I left the house and started walking to San Jose Hospital on Santa Clara and 14th Street. It wasn't far; we were used to walking to the Jose Theater and Alum Rock Park. They were both about four miles from our house.

On the way to the hospital, I thought of the two times I had been there as a patient. When I was only four years old, a car hit me. The other time was when I had my tonsils removed. I asked Mom if it was going to hurt; she said no. She was right; it didn't hurt at all. The most memorable events of this hospitalization were waking up to ice cream and, of course, Mom by my side. Now it was my turn to be by her side.

Arriving at the hospital, I knew I had to find my mother's room without being seen. I had a plan. If I was asked how old I was, my answer would be, "Sixteen years old," because no one under sixteen was allowed in the rooms with the patients. The hospital staff thought we would contract the sickness of the patient. I thought this was a stupid rule because I didn't think it was possible to catch my mother's illness. I reasoned that Mom should still be in the emergency department because it was too soon for her to be taken to her own room.

The emergency department was on 14th Street, and the main lobby was on Santa Clara Street. I saw my father's Cadillac parked on 14th Street where there was only room to park on one side of the road. I entered the emergency doors and stepped into the large waiting room. There was a counter with big doors next to it. Behind the counter was a nurse. There were a lot of people waiting. Some were standing, and some were sitting. I didn't know if I should ask about Mom or just walk through the big doors to see if I could spot Dad or locate her.

I decided to walk in through the big doors. When I tried to open them, I found they were locked. I realized it was necessary to wait for the next person to come through them; and when they did, I would enter. I stood by the doors and waited, looking around at all the people. Everyone looked sad and drained.

The doors finally opened, and a man walked through them. As he went by me, I stepped through the doorway, walking fast and not looking at the nurse, hoping she didn't notice me.

I was out of sight of the nurse behind the counter. My good plan had worked. I thought I was home free when I heard, "May I help you, young man?" It was another nurse. She was walking toward me from one of the side hallways.

"Yes. I'm looking for my mother," I answered in a soft tone, trying to sound innocent.

"Your mother? Is she here as a patient?"

"Yeah, she just got here a little while ago. They brought her here in an ambulance."

"Come back to the counter with me. I'll check."

When we reached the counter and the big doors, she instructed, "You can go around the other side of the counter, and I'll check for you."

I walked around through the big doors and stepped in front of the counter. The nurse was looking for the roster. She found it in the maze of papers on the bottom part of the counter and asked, "What is your mother's name?"

"Mildred Rodriguez."

"No, I don't show anyone here by that name. Sorry."
"You must be wrong. She is here."
"No, maybe they sent her home. What was wrong with her?"

Just as I was going to answer, I saw Dad walking toward me. He was walking with his head down. He then looked up at the nurse's station and saw me. "Arturo! Mijo, what are you doing here? I told you to stay home."

"I know you did, Dad; but I couldn't! I had to come."

The nurse observed my father as he spoke. She then knew who my mother was. She had already talked to Dad. "Oh, this is your father," she said to me.

I didn't pay any attention to her, awaiting my father's reply. I wanted to know what he was going to tell me about coming to the hospital; but, more importantly, I wanted to know how Mom was doing. Quietly I waited to see what he was going to say, wishing that he would tell me my mother wasn't dead. I thought and prayed, "I hope. I hope. Please, God, don't let him tell me . . ."

"Your mother is OK. They are working on her."

"What do you mean they are working on her, Dad?"

"Arturito, let's go and sit down in the waiting room."

The waiting room was part of where we were standing. It was a large room with many sofas made of steel and colored, padded cushions. Most of the sofas were occupied with people who were waiting for word about their loved ones. We walked over to a couple of vacant seats. Dad put his hand out for me to sit down first; he sat next to me. He had never treated me as an adult.

My father spoke to me in Spanish, "Arturo, your mother is very sick. The doctor talked to me just a few minutes ago. He said he didn't know if she will survive. Right now they are pumping her stomach."

"Did he say Mom was going to die? Did he say that?"

"They do not really know yet. She took a lot of tranquilizers, a whole bottle. The doctor is doing the best he can."

"Did she take enough to kill her?"

"Yes, Arturo. They will also do other tests. Your mother was very depressed."

I was all ears, listening to every word. I asked, "They can't tell you if Mom is going to be all right for sure, right?" I knew the answer, but I was asking again anyway.

"No, they can not. We just have to wait to see. Unless they know something already and are not telling me."

"Do you think so?"

"Who knows? I do not know what they are thinking."

I knew I was asking too many questions for Dad, but I had to ask. I wanted to know all the details about Mom. "Do you think all the fighting had anything to do with it?" I also knew the answer to this but I was asking anyway.

Dad grabbed his hair and pulled it back, in the same manner as he had when he was standing behind the ambulance earlier. "I do not know! I do not know what to think. I love your mother very much, Arturo."

I sat and wondered, "Was this true?" I recalled the way he was running around in a panic at home when he saw the way she was. "But why does he go out so much and leave her? And why would he get so angry at her all those years?" We both sat there during the next few minutes, thinking to ourselves.

"What did you think when you saw her? Did she tell you anything?"

"Si, she said she could not move. She said she had no strength. Then she said, 'Oh, my babies.' She does not want to leave you ninos (children), Arturo. She does not want to! She does not want to leave any of us. She loves us all very much." My mother was ready to die but when Victor stepped by her, it was then that she thought of her children and told my father what she had done.

Dad was a very proud man. He didn't like things to happen over which he had no control. He was the kind of person who didn't like to admit when he was wrong, always wanting to have things done his way. He insisted on total respect and loyalty from his family. If this didn't happen, we were in big trouble.

"Jose Edmundo Rodriguez?" the doctor called.

Dad and I rose. My father had an expression that indicated he expected to receive bad news. "I am Jose Rodriguez!"

Dad took three big steps to meet the doctor and said, "You can call me Jose."

"Hello, Mr. Rodriguez. I am Dr. Jones. I know you already spoke with Dr. Olson. He and I are working together. Apparently your wife is extremely ill. Do you know exactly what caused her to take this medication?"

"No. I have the bottle here," he said as he pulled out the empty container from his pocket and handed it to the doctor. "It has her name on it. She must have gotten it from her personal doctor last week."

"How is she, doctor? How does she look to you? Do you think she will make it?"

"Well, Mr. Rodriguez, that is hard to say. It depends on how much of this medication made it into her system. It is difficult to say right now. The only thing that will determine the outcome is time. Do you have children?"

"Yes," Dad replied sadly, sensing why he was asking. "We have four children."

"I see. Too bad. I will do everything I can, Mr. Rodriguez."

"Doctor, do whatever it takes to save my wife. I do not care how much it costs! I will pay!"

"I wish I could tell you that I can save your wife. However, unfortunately there is not much else I can do. It is in God's hands now. We just have to wait."

"How long before we know, Doctor?"

"I cannot answer that either. Time will tell. All I can tell you is for every hour she is alive, thank God for it."

"We will be moving her up to a room now. She will have a nurse with her twenty-four hours. Hopefully, she will be out of danger soon."

"Thank you, doctor. I will be here with her."

"You should go home and get some rest. I know your other children need you. I will instruct the nurses to call you if there is any change whatsoever in her condition."

"No, Doctor, I cannot leave my wife. The children at home will be fine. There will be family there with them. My wife needs me now, and I am going to be here for her."

"All right, Mr. Rodriguez; however, you will have to sleep in the waiting room. We cannot put up a bed for you in her room," Dr. Jones explained rudely. He didn't like the idea that Dad was going to be spending the nights at the hospital.

"This is all right. I can sleep sitting on a chair. I do not have a problem with that."

"Mr. Rodriguez, suit yourself. I will tell the nurse. If you would like to go to her room before we take her upstairs, you may. However, she is in a coma and will not know you are there."

"Thank you, Dr. Jones."

The doctor turned and walked away.

Dad started to follow him to Mom's room. I took a few steps behind him. The doctor turned, observed me, and questioned, "I'm sorry, young man, but how old are you?"

I was disappointed the doctor noticed me. I wanted to lie, but I knew Dad wouldn't approve of it. "I'm thirteen years old."

"You know, you have to be sixteen to enter the rooms here at this hospital. That's the rule at San Jose Hospital."

"OK," I said and stopped. Dad and the doctor kept walking until they were out of sight. I went back to where we were sitting and sat back down.

In ten minutes I looked up as someone came barging in from outside through the large doors of the emergency department. It was Uncle Ben.

"Uncle Ben! Hi!" I stood up to embrace him, happy to see him. Behind him were Eddie, Tita, Victor, and many uncles and aunts.

"Hi, Mijo," he said as he embraced me. Uncle Ben was a very good uncle. I had always loved him very much. "Where is your mother, Arthur?"

"She's in a room back there somewhere. They wouldn't let me go in because I'm too young. But my dad is there with her. The doctor just came out to talk to my dad."

"What did the doctor say, Mijo?" Uncle Ben asked, his eyes squinting, concentrating on what I was going to say, wanting to know if I knew the prognosis of his sister.

"He said he didn't know if my mom is going to live. We have to wait to see. He said it might take time. For every hour she is alive, we should be grateful."

"The doctor told you that?"

"Well, he told my dad that; but I was standing right there."

Uncle Ben shook his head in contempt because the doctor had made these comments in front of me. "Stupid doctor!"

"I hope my mom is going to be all right."

"Don't worry, Arthur; she will. I just know it. I'm going to go and look for her. Did the doctor say what room she is in?"

"No, I don't know."

As Uncle Ben started to walk away, he said, "That's OK; I'll find out. I'll ask a nurse."

"I don't think they'll let you in, Uncle Ben."

He turned and answered, "Who won't let me in? They can't keep your uncle Ben out of his sister's room! Don't worry, Mijo; I'll see your mom!" Uncle Ben was one of those men who loved to fight. If things didn't go his way, he would take the first swing. My other uncle, Uncle Joe, was the same way.

As I observed my aunts and other uncles gathering around to embrace me, my mind drifted back to the knife fight.

Chapter Thirteen

The Knife Fight

I was eight years old and living on Virginia Place. Dad went out on Friday nights to play cards with his friends. He enjoyed doing this because he would always win. Some of the money he won he would keep, and the other part of it he would spend on buying beer for his friends. Dad was the kind of man who could drink beer all night long; and if someone spoke to him, they wouldn't be able to tell he was drinking. Once he played cards with his friends until dawn. Afterward, they counted 63 empty beer cans where Dad had been sitting.

Dad wasn't a fighter; but if trouble came his way, he took care of business. When he was very young, he liked to fight. Now that he had children and a job that he enjoyed, he knew better.

Uncle Ben, my mother's younger brother, enjoyed fighting when he was drinking. Once he had two beers, it was time for Uncle Ben to look for someone to fight. It was said he would occasionally lose a fight, but that was seldom.

Uncle Ben was a married man; however, he enjoyed having pretty girlfriends. He claimed he loved his wife, but that didn't stop him from playing the field. Aunt Fammy and Uncle Ben put up with each other a lot. They both had their faults. They had two children, Benny and little Linda.

Dad took Uncle Ben with him to play cards. Uncle Ben wasn't a player who won, but he enjoyed going. Sometimes when he went with Dad and his friends to play cards, he would take some of the men from his job. They were set up to lose their money because Dad was such a good player.

There was a problem. In a short while after having a couple of beers, Uncle Ben would become loud and want to fight Dad's friends. After a few times when this occurred, Dad was asked by his buddies not to take Uncle Ben when they went out drinking.

On one particular evening Mom was working at the cannery, and Dad was home with us. Dad was in the shower getting ready to go out on this late Saturday night. Uncle Ben pulled up in his new pink Plymouth with the big fins in the back. He loved his car and thought the color pink was cool because all the women liked it. I thought it was corny for a man to have a pink car.

We children were in the living room watching TV. The front door was open. "Hey, kids!" we heard.

"Hi, Uncle Ben!" Eddie responded, standing to greet him. I followed Eddie and so did Tita. Tita was a pretty little girl with curls all around her head.

As he was embracing us, he asked, "Where is your daddy?" Uncle Ben was wearing black pants, a red shirt with long sleeves with the cuffs rolled up, and a black vest.

I answered Uncle Ben, "He's in the shower. I think he's getting ready to go out."

"He is? Good," Uncle Ben replied as he walked down the hallway toward the bathroom. Once there, he banged on the door and yelled, "Hey, Joe! Joe!"

"Yeah, Ben?" Dad answered.

"Hurry, because I'm going with you. I don't have all day!"

"Ay, ay, ay, Benny. ¿Qué trais (what's wrong with you)?" Even though we were at the other side of the house, we could hear Dad; and he sounded irritated. I was hoping Dad didn't become angry because we knew how he was when that happened.

Uncle Ben had always been respectful with Dad. However, lately he had been a little demanding with him because he knew Dad wasn't a fighter as he was. He thought he could push Dad around. Dad put up with Uncle Ben because he was my mother's brother. He was seven years older than Uncle Ben.

Uncle Ben came back to the living room, "So what are you kids watching?"

"A movie, Uncle Ben. It's a good one," Tita answered.

I heard the shower stop. So did Uncle Ben. He went back to the door to the bathroom. "Joe, do you have any beer in this house?"

"No, Benny." Dad wasn't saying too much. He sounded as if he didn't want Uncle Ben to go with him.

"Well, then hurry, Joe! I need a beer!"

Uncle Ben came back into the living room and sat on the sofa. He asked Tita to pass him the telephone. As he waited, he talked to what sounded like a woman, laughing and smiling as he talked in a low voice, slumped down on the couch.

Dad stayed in the bathroom for a few more minutes, shaving and getting ready. In a short time he came out and walked to his bedroom. Uncle Ben yelled out, "About time! OK, Joe, ready?"

Dad didn't answer. He didn't like being spoken to in the way Uncle Ben was talking to him. Uncle Ben hung up the telephone and walked over to look out the screen door. He stepped into the kitchen and opened the refrigerator door, putting his hand in and taking something out with his fingers. He stuck whatever it was in his mouth.

"Arthur, what time does your mom come home?"

"I'm not sure, Uncle Ben. Tonight."

"I know that, Mijo! What time tonight do you think?" He said in a low voice, "Do you think I'm dumb?"

"No, Uncle Ben, I don't think that."

Dad stepped out of his bedroom. He appeared clean and fresh with a couple of drops of water on his forehead. He looked at Eddie, tilted his head up, and asked, "Where is your tio (uncle)?"

Eddie moved his head in the direction of the kitchen, lifted his hand, pointed, and answered, "In there, Dad."

We all knew things were not going to go well. We kids observed how Uncle Ben was speaking to Dad, knowing Dad might really get upset with him. If this happened, then Dad would really become angry. I wondered how much Dad could take before this occurred.

"Benny! Come on, if you want to go with me!" Dad demanded harshly.

"About time!" Uncle Ben exclaimed as he came back into the living room, chewing whatever he took from the refrigerator again.

Dad stood by the front door. "Niños, I will be back in a little while. Be good! Don't make a mess in here. Eddie, take care of them!" Dad demanded in the strong way that he always spoke to us.

"OK, Dad, I will," he answered, trying to pay attention to the movie and Dad at the same time.

Dad stepped out through the front screen door, not saying anything else to Uncle Ben. Uncle Ben followed, not saying anything to Dad nor to us. At this point it didn't seem either one of them really wanted to go out with the other.

I climbed on the sofa and looked out the window at them. They stopped walking before getting into Dad's green Pontiac with the Pontiac Indian face on the hood. Dad appeared as if he was scolding Uncle Ben, shaking his finger at his nose. It looked as if Dad was telling him to be careful the way he was speaking to him. Uncle Ben stood and listened as if he was taking whatever counsel Dad was giving him. I also thought Dad was telling Uncle Ben that he had better behave himself when they went to see Dad's friends.

They both climbed into the car. Dad started the engine and backed out of the driveway. As Dad was looking back for traffic, which there was none because we were at a dead-end street, I saw that he was still speaking. Dad had a hard expression.

We sat in the living room for about an hour. I told Eddie I was going to make some popcorn, so we could enjoy the movie better. He agreed but reminded me not to make a big mess in the kitchen. I told him I never made messes.

"Arthur, you're crazy. You always make messes!" Eddie replied sarcastically.

Just as I took the big pot out and put it on the stove, I heard a car drive into the driveway. I knew it couldn't be Dad and Uncle Ben because they just left not more than an hour ago. I stopped what I was doing and went to the window. Sure enough, it was them. I saw Dad get out of the car; he didn't look happy. Just before he entered the house, I stood from the sofa and sat on the floor.

The door opened, "Hi, Dad." It was a rule in our house that we always had to greet Dad and Mom. If we didn't, we would get into trouble. Big trouble!

Eddie turned and said, "Hi, Dad!" Tita and little Victor stood up and gave Dad a hug. He didn't answer any of us and appeared agitated. Uncle Ben entered behind Dad and said, "Hey, Joe, let's go back! Come on, Joe! Let's go back!"

Dad didn't say anything. He marched into the living room and, just as he was going to go down the hallway, Uncle Ben yelled and repeated, "José! I said, Let's go back there!"

Dad stopped and looked at Uncle Ben with an expression that could kill. He demanded, "Benny, go home! Just go home, Benny!"

"I'm not going home, Joe! Hey, if I can't fight your friends, then I want to fight you!"

"Benny, you are loco! Just go home and sleep your two beers off."

Uncle Ben didn't like the remark. He knew Dad could drink a lot, and he couldn't. "I'm not going home until I have me a good fight. And if you're not going to take me back to fight one of your sissy friends, then we, you and me, are going to fight!"

Dad continued to walk down the hallway. Uncle Ben followed and continued to harass him. We were all shocked that he wanted to fight with Dad. None of us said anything. We just listened.

I heard the bathroom door close and then heard banging on the door. "Hey, Joe, come out of there! Hurry!" Uncle Ben yelled as he continued to bang on the door.

"Benny, go home! My friends and I don't want to fight you! You are not worth it. Just go home, Benny!"

"Come on, Joe! You chicken? You are just plain old chicken, Joe!" Uncle Ben blared out, as he gave a sarcastic laugh. "Chicken, Joe! You're chicken just like your sissy friends!"

The bathroom door opened, and Dad came out. He stepped right past Uncle Ben and proceeded to his bedroom. Uncle Ben was right behind him. "Come on, Joe! Scared to fight with me? You know I'll take you easy!"

Dad stopped right where we could see him before he entered his bedroom. In a low tone and stoned faced, Dad said, "Benny, I said to just go home! Do you understand? I don't want to fight with you!"

"Hey, I didn't want to fight with you either; but you wouldn't let me fight your sissy friends. Now I have to fight with you!"

"Benny, just go home while it's still safe for you!"

"Safe? You're nothing but a chicken, Joe! That's it, you're just a big chicken!"

Dad stepped into his bedroom and slammed the door right in Uncle Ben's face. Uncle Ben didn't like this at all.

"Hey, Joe, what do you think you are doing, chicken! Hey, sissy, what's wrong with you?"

We all sat there in the living room hoping Uncle Ben would shut up before he really upset Dad. Uncle Ben started to bang on the bedroom door. He yelled, "Come on, Joe! Come . . ."

Dad opened the door. He just stood there looking at Uncle Ben. After a few seconds he said, "OK, Benny, you want to die? We'll fight then!"

Uncle Ben stood there with an expression as if he knew he might have gone too far. In a few, short seconds he replied, "Yeah, Joe, I want to fight. I know I can take you easy!"

"OK, Benny, you asked for it. We are really going to fight. You know, Benny, I don't fight to play. When I fight, it is to win, forever! So you will never come back to fight again! Now you put yourself into a real fight, a fight for your life! You are not going to get out of this so easy, Benny. Come on!" Dad ordered as he marched toward the kitchen.

"Hey, Joe, do you want to fight in the kitchen or outside?"

All of us stood up and were no longer interested in the movie we were watching. We didn't want to see Dad and Uncle Ben fight. I wished Mom would come home from work; she could stop what was happening.

I had never before seen Uncle Ben act this way with Dad. Just before Dad stepped into the kitchen, he told Uncle Ben, "Benny, go outside and wait for me! I will be right out! I will get the knives!"

"Oh, no!" I thought. I didn't want Dad and Uncle Ben to fight with knives. I didn't want my father to die on that day!

Uncle Ben stood there, not believing what he heard. I knew he never expected to fight Dad with knives. He didn't say anything more and had an expression as if he was thinking, "What in the heck did I get myself into?"

Dad stepped into the kitchen; we followed him to see what he was getting. We didn't believe Dad was really getting knives to fight Uncle Ben.

Uncle Ben stood by the front door. He wasn't saying anything anymore. I figured he was getting cold feet about taking on Dad. He thought Dad was going to fight with his bare hands, but he had other plans.

Uncle Ben walked out to the front of the house. We saw Dad get two of the biggest knives we had. As he stepped out of the kitchen, he walked by us without saying anything. At the same time we all said, "No Dad! Don't fight Uncle Ben, Dad!"

Dad didn't look our way but kept right on walking through the living room and out the front door. We followed him.

Uncle Ben was standing on the front lawn, waiting to see what Dad was going to do. It was dark outside. We always left our front porch light on once it became dark.

"¡Bueno, Benny! ¿Listo (ready)? You want to fight, huh? You are going to have a fight for your life!" Dad barked angrily, very upset at all the badgering uncle Ben had directed toward him.

Dad stepped to the center of the grass and threw both knives hard into the ground. It seemed he knew his knives well. When he threw them, they both stuck into the ground, right on target at the same time.

Uncle Ben wasn't saying anything. He looked surprised that Dad was so upset and had an expression as if he didn't understand Dad's anger, thinking it wouldn't come to this.

Tita and Victor were crying. We all knew Dad meant business. He walked back to Uncle Ben and said, "OK, Benny, we both have had it. One of us is going to the electric chair, and the other one will die here!"

All four of us were begging Dad and Uncle Ben not to fight. "Uncle Ben! Why did you start a fight with my dad? Now look what you did!" I hollered.

Uncle Ben looked at me. He had a sad expression and looked as if he knew he had made a big mistake by taunting Dad.

"¿Listo (Ready), Benny? When I say three, get ready, Benny! This is your life! Let the best man win! You want to fight, huh?" Dad said with his sarcastic laugh, "Ha, ha, ha, ha." He continued, "Now you are going to know what a real fight is. This is not a fist fight but a fight for blood! Now, when I count to three, go for your knife fast because I'm not stopping! It is going to be you or me. I want to live longer and make it to the electric chair, so I'm getting my knife and using it!"

"Dad, don't fight Uncle Ben!" I yelled. "You're going to kill him. Uncle Ben, go home! Go home!"

Eddie was yelling, "Dad, don't fight Uncle Ben! Dad!"

Tita and Victor were sobbing.

"Come on, Benny! Are you ready?" Dad asked, facing him.

Uncle Ben looked as if he was in shock and didn't answer. He put his hands in his pockets as if he was cold on that warm, summer evening.

Some of the neighbors were coming out of their houses because they heard the yelling and wondered what was happening. Dad turned toward the knives in the center of the lawn.

"¡Uno (one)!" Dad yelled.

"No, Dad! Please!" I didn't want to see either my father or my uncle Ben die and didn't know what to do. I couldn't stand to watch them be killed and ran down the side of the house to the back yard in a panic, not wanting to deal with the situation. As I left, I heard everyone yelling and crying. The back yard was dark. I couldn't hear anything that was going on in the front from where I now stood. I didn't know what to do and wanted to run to the front to try to stop them from killing one another.

"Please, God! Please! If there is a God, help them so they don't kill each other."

Walking to one side of the yard then to the other side in the dark, I wondered what was happening. Had someone died yet? Waiting for a few more minutes to hear the sirens screaming down Virginia Place, I stepped back to the side of the house to see if I could hear anything. "No sounds," I thought.

I moved slowly toward the front of the house. All was quiet. "Had someone died yet?" I asked myself. When I approached the front corner of the house, I didn't see anyone or hear anything. "Where did everybody go?" I asked myself. The neighborhood was also quiet. I was only gone for a few minutes, and it seemed as if nothing had ever happened.

I scanned the street; Uncle Ben's car was gone. I looked into the living room window and saw Eddie, Tita, and Victor watching TV again. I felt as if I were in the Twilight Zone.

I stepped into the house and asked, "What happened?"

"Eddie looked up at me from the carpet where he was sitting and answered, "Nothing."

"But what happened with Dad and Uncle Ben?" I asked, confused.

"Nothing, Arthur," Eddie answered again. Tita and Victor were concentrating on the movie they were watching.

"But what happened to Uncle Ben? His car isn't here."

Eddie looked up at me and explained, "He didn't go for the knife. When Dad counted to three, Uncle Ben turned around and walked to his car without saying anything. Then he started it up and left. Dad picked up the knives and told us to come into the house."

"Where is Dad?"

"He went to bed. He's in his room."

From that day forward Uncle Ben always spoke to Dad with respect and never asked to go out with him again. Even though Uncle Ben had a problem with drinking and having other girlfriends, we all loved him very much.

Chapter Fourteen

The Wait

Our family was sitting in the waiting room expecting word of my mother's condition. Aunt Annabel left the room to look for Mom. In a little while she returned and told us she had been moved upstairs. There was a waiting room down the hall from where Mom was; therefore, we all proceeded upstairs. We crowded into the small room; some of our family stood in the outside hall because there wasn't enough room for everyone.

It was decided that some of the family would go home and take Tita and Victor with them. Eddie wanted to stay a little longer. Every little while Uncle Ben or Aunt Annabel would come out to the waiting room to inform us of the latest developments, which were not very much at this time. The doctor told them it could be days before there was any change. I told my aunts that the last time I saw Mom she really appeared pale and motionless. Uncle Ben, Aunt Annabel, and everyone else looked worried.

As the hours passed, more of the family decided to leave and come back in the morning. Uncle Ben told them he would call if there was even a slight change in Mom's condition.

Soon it was only Uncle Ben, Aunt Annabel, and I who stayed at the hospital. The hours went by slowly. Dad was staying in the room with Mom most of the time; he didn't want to leave her side. Occasionally I would sneak into the room and hold Mom's hand and talk to her.

"Young man, I step out of the room and as soon as I do, you come in. You know you are not supposed to be in here," the nurse told me.

"I know, but I had to come and hold my mom's hand. I miss her."

"I know you do. But if you're in here and the doctor sees you, I'll get into trouble. So you have to stay out in the waiting room."

The nurse was nice and spoke to me in a kind way. Sometimes when she would catch me in the room with Mom, she would let me stay for a few minutes.

Later that night Uncle Ben and Aunt Annabel went home.

I spent that first night in the waiting room. Despite what the doctor told Dad, he was able to sleep in a chair next to Mom. Once in a while Dad would come in and sit with me. We talked about a lot of things.

"Dad, what exactly did Mom say when you saw her on the floor?" I asked. He had already told me, but I wanted to hear it again.

"Pues, Tita and Victor were playing in the living room. Your mother came out of the bedroom for something. Victor ran right in front of her and almost knocked her down. After that I noticed she didn't look right. Then she told me, 'Something is not right. I don't feel. . .' She went back into Tita's bedroom. The next thing I knew, she was collapsed on the floor."

"Oh, she told you like that? Dad, what do you think is wrong with her?"

"I do not know, Mijo. I do not know."

The first night went by with no change in Mom's condition. The doctor came by early in the morning to see how she was doing. He spoke with Dad and told him there was nothing they could do but wait. Dad understood. He even came to the waiting room and explained it to me. He said there was nothing anyone could do. Dad never said anything about God helping Mom. He didn't really believe in God. He wouldn't let Mom teach us about religion or take us to any church because he said he wanted us to make our own decisions about religion when we became adults.

Early in the morning Uncle Ben came to be with Mom for awhile. Uncle Ben stepped into the waiting room; he looked fresh and rested. "Benny," Dad greeted, happy to see Uncle Ben.

"Joe, how are you? Did you get any sleep at all?"

"No, not too good. But that is all right." Dad looked at me and continued, "Arturo didn't either. I know he is tired."

"Arturo, you should go home and rest," Dad said as if he was feeling sorry for me.

"Dad, I don't need to rest. I'm fine. I want to stay here with Mom."

"But, Mijo, there is nothing you can do. You might as well go home, rest, take a shower, and come back later."

When Dad said this, I thought to myself, "What if I go and Mom dies? If I left, I would never be able to live with myself. I can't go. As long as there is danger, I have to stay!"

"No, Dad, I have to stay. I can't leave Mom. If anything happens to her, then . . ."

"OK, Mijo, you can stay. But you know what the doctor said. It might take a few days for your mother to get well."

"That's all right, Dad. I'll stay a few days."

Uncle Ben was standing at the doorway of the waiting room, listening to our conversation. He asked, "Arthur, do you want me to take you home so you can shower? I will bring you right back. You will feel a lot better if you shower. I think it's going to be a long day."

"OK, Uncle Ben, that sounds like a good idea. I'll go, but I want to come right back."

Dad put his arm around my shoulder and told me that was good. "Mijo, you are acting like a man; and that is very good."

When we walked out of the hospital, the morning was quiet. There were no cars on the streets. It was going to be a warm day and felt fresh outside. I was glad Dad had talked me into going home to shower. I needed it.

Uncle Ben took me home and didn't mind doing it. I wasn't accustomed to being treated this way by grown-ups.

Once we were at my house, Uncle Ben told me he was going to drive home and would be back in a half-hour. He lived in the small town of Milpitas about eight miles away.

I took my shower; it felt good. No one was home at the time; and I didn't know where Eddie, Mildred, and Victor were at that moment.

Shortly thereafter, Uncle Ben yelled out from the front of the house, "Arthur, I'm back. I'll be in the front yard waiting for you."

When I was done, I went to the front yard to where Uncle Ben was waiting for me. I had changed into a long-sleeve, Pendleton shirt and Levi's pants. I took with me a light green sweater for the night.

"OK, Mijo, are you ready?"

"Yeah, Uncle Ben, I'm ready."

We stepped into his car and drove away. As he drove, I thought of the day before when I saw Mom and the way she looked. It was the saddest day of my life, and I hoped there wasn't going to be an even sadder one. I never wanted anything like this to happen again. My eyes became teary. The tears started to fall as I looked out the window. I didn't want Uncle Ben to see me cry.

"It's going to be OK, Arthur. Don't worry. If your mamma were going to die, she would have died already. It can only go one way, and that is for the better. Don't worry, Mijo," Uncle Ben said soothingly. I could tell he wanted to cry also. He loved Mom and was close to her as well. All of Mom's family always visited each other regularly.

As we were driving to the hospital, I remembered going to Uncle Ben and Uncle Willie's houses on many occasions. All the family would gather there and have parties. I recalled looking in the house at all the grown-ups who were having fun. When they had parties and my grandfather was there, he would make a lot of noise while he danced. He stomped his feet on the floor as if he were trying to crash through it. Also, I would spot Mom in the crowd. I remembered how beautiful she always appeared, even though she was wearing her everyday clothes.

We pulled up to the hospital entry, and I thanked Uncle Ben again. When I returned to the third floor, Dad was sitting in the same spot I left him.

Even though I didn't sleep all night, I wasn't sleepy. Dad appeared as if he really needed some sleep and a shower. He looked tired!

He glanced up as I stepped into the waiting room, "Arturito, how are the muchachos (boys) and Tita?"

"No one was home when I went, Dad," I answered.

"Benny, if you are going to be here for awhile, I'll take Arturo to go eat. Did you eat at home, Arturo?"

"No, I didn't eat."

"Oh yeah, Joe, no problem. Go and eat. I'll be here. Take your time," Uncle Ben replied sincerely.

"Vamonos (Let's go), Arturo. We will get something to eat," Dad stated as he affectionately put his hand on my head.

We walked two blocks to 12th and Santa Clara Streets to a small restaurant. The waitress took us to a table by the front window. Dad asked me what I wanted; I told him pancakes, eggs, and potatoes.

As Dad was giving the waitress our order, I looked outside and saw a few cars starting to pass. "People are starting to come alive this morning. I wish Mom would come alive."

I hated the feeling of being away from her like this. I wanted her back and now! I wanted to hear her soft voice telling me she loved me.

Mom rarely became angry with us. I remember one time when we were visiting my grandmother. Mom became really upset with me and brought out the belt. She started hitting me with it. When Mom hit, it was nothing compared to Dad's beatings. She became really angry as she hit me. Later, when it was all over, she felt really upset with herself for losing her patience. Mom was always such a loving person.

The waitress brought my orange juice and Dad's coffee. I took a sip of it. The orange juice tasted good. I thought to myself, "Here I am with Dad talking as if I were his friend." This was the first time I could remember being in this situation with him, when it was just the two of us. I didn't know what to say, feeling odd being with him as he told me stories about himself.

"Mijo, when I was young like you, I was already a man."

Dad always reminded us of what he went through when he was young. We always just listened, never asking questions. Now that I was getting along with him and we were talking, I thought I would ask about something I always wanted to know.

"Dad, you got shot in the head when you were young? What happened? How did it happen?"

"Well, Mijo, I was sixteen years old. I was going to boarding school in San Cristobal de Las Casas, about a two-hour drive from my town." San Cristobal de Las Casas was in the state of Chiapas, the most southern state of Mexico. "I had a problem with this guy who was from another area. One morning I was having my frijoles and tortillas in a small restaurant when this guy came from behind me and put his gun to the side of my head."

"Wow, what did you do?" I asked, giving Dad my full attention.

"This guy Tómas held the gun to my head and had his other arm around my neck. I could not move. He told me, 'Now let us see what kind of man you are!'"

"I laughed and said, 'Oh yeah, you have a gun to my head; and I am eating with utensils in my hands.'"

"Were you scared, Dad?" I asked, wide-eyed and waiting for the rest of the story.

"No, Arturo, I was a little worried. I had my gun in my belt, but I could not reach for it. I knew if I did he would pull the trigger."

"You had a gun?" I asked, really surprised.

"Sí, everybody had guns in those days. We did not feel safe without them."

"So, what happened?"

"I knew I had to make my move right at that moment. With all of my might, I pushed up with my feet. At the same time I dropped my knife and fork," Dad said as he acted it out with his utensils in his hands. "With my left hand I reached up to get a hold of Tomas' gun; and with my right hand I reached down to grab a hold of my gun in my belt, hoping Tómas would lose control of the situation. My hand was only inches away from my gun when I saw a fireball explode next to my head. I felt as if my face and jaw had been ripped apart by the blast. There was a great numbness that overcame my face and the side of my head. I was blinded from the explosion. The bullet ripped through the side of my face next to my ear," he explained as he pointed to his face, "and then on the upper part of my jaw. It came out on the other side of my face through my lower jaw.

"Man, Dad, that was bad," I said, not thinking. Dad had always become upset and sometimes even hit us when we used the word "man" with him. He thought it was very disrespectful to address one's parents in this way. It didn't appear as if he noticed my using the word at that moment.

"Then what happened, Dad?"

"I could not see anything. I struggled to turn my body around, holding onto Tómas. I had a hold of Tómas' gun. He did not mean for the gun to go off. His plan was to frighten me and make me beg for my life. Tómas was trying to push me away so that he could make his getaway. Blood was everywhere."

The waitress came to the table and asked if we wanted anything else. Dad answered, "No, we are fine. You can get our check ready."

She said, "OK," picked up some of our plates, and walked away.

Dad continued, "I was able to pull the gun away from Tómas. As I did, Tomas grabbed for it. It got loose, and the gun fell to the ground. I reached up with both hands and choked Tómas with all of my might. My legs were starting to collapse as I tried to tighten my grip on Tómas' neck. I was in pain by then, but I still put all of my strength in trying to fight Tómas as much as I could before I passed out. Tomas was fighting for oxygen. He did not know from where or how I was getting all my strength after he shot me."

"This sounds like a movie, Dad."

Dad laughed and said, "No, Arturo, it was no movie. It was real!"

"Then what happened?"

"As I was struggling with Tómas, I remembered the gun in my belt. I let go of his neck and reached for it. Tómas gasped for oxygen. I reached for the gun and aimed it at Tómas' face, pulling the trigger. It did not go off. I pulled the trigger again."

As Dad was speaking, I was in a trance as if I were right there with him. Dad took a drink of his coffee and continued, "Tómas looked as if he knew he was going to die. Again, the gun did not go off. I turned the gun around; and with the butt of the gun, I started to bang on his head over and over again as hard as I could. I had to keep hitting him. I knew that if I did not knock him out and I gave him another chance he was going to kill me. So I did not stop hitting him. Finally I felt Tómas getting weak. I wanted to do as much damage to him as I could before I blacked out. Someone in the restaurant yelled out, 'Stop! Stop!' That was the last thing I remember."

I was shocked that my father had been shot like this. I always knew that it happened, but never had so much detail. "Does it hurt you now, Dad?"

The waitress walked by and left the check on the table.

Dad laughed, "No, Arturo. It has been a long time. But I cannot feel the side of my face. That's why sometimes when you see me eating and there's food on my lip or on my face it's because I have no feeling there."

I always noticed this about Dad and wondered why he didn't use his napkin when he needed it.

We sat and talked a little more about other things. We spoke about Mom, both saying we wished things would change and that she would come out of the coma.

"All right, Arturo, let's go back to the hospital," Dad said.

My father had never been so friendly with me. I wondered to myself as he was speaking, when this ordeal with my mother was over, if he would continue to be this way. I sure hoped so! It was fun!

"OK, Mijo, let's go back to the hospital," he stated again as he stood and reached for the check the waitress had left on the table.

"OK, Dad," I acknowledged as I stood. "I hope Mom comes out of her coma fast. I really miss her."

"Sí, Arturo. So do I."

"Dad, you said you weren't going to Mexico after all? That's what I heard you say. Are you?"

"No, I do not think so, Arturo. I think if I do go I am going to take all of you with me."

I didn't like his answer because I sure didn't want to go to Mexico to live. We had been to Mexico City when I was younger. I had also been to a border town many times to visit my uncle, but to move? "No way!" I thought.

I didn't reply to what Dad said. He was also silent. Maybe he was waiting to see how I was going to respond. To Dad it wasn't going to make a difference if I wanted to go to Mexico or not. If he wanted to go, he would take us; and that was it.

On arriving back at the hospital, we found Uncle Ben with Mom. I didn't know why, but there was now a sofa right outside of Mom's hospital room. "This is cool," I thought, knowing I could now be closer to her.

Dad went into the room, and I sat on the sofa. In a little while Uncle Ben came out and saw me sitting on the couch. "Arthur, how do you like what I got for you? I made them bring a sofa, so you can be here right next to the room!"

"Man, Uncle Ben, how did you do that? This is really cool!" I said smiling happily at Uncle Ben.

"Well, there was this beautiful nurse who walked by. I started talking to her. After awhile, because she liked me, she had some guys bring over this sofa for us. I'm telling you, Arthur, these women really go for me!"

I started laughing as he said this and replied, "I know they do,

Uncle Ben. You got it, man!"

It seemed every month Uncle Ben had a different girlfriend. During this time he was separated from Aunt Fammy a lot. I never knew if the reason for their troubled marriage was because of the other women; however, I figured it was.

Uncle Ben sat with me, and we talked for a little while. In about a half-hour, other aunts and uncles arrived to see Mom. I stood and let them sit down. At times it seemed we had a mob of people outside of Mom's room. Periodically during the day there was a lot of family to see her; sometimes there was none, just Dad, Uncle Ben, and me. Dad and I talked a lot during those hours. He told me things I never understood. I even became brave enough to ask Dad about his girlfriends.

"Arturo, you know men cannot stay with only one woman all the time. I know you don't understand now because you are so young. But I know you will see it when you get older. I know because you are my son, and you have the same blood as I do," Dad said sincerely.

When he told me this, I knew he was right, right that I didn't understand. I wondered if he was right about understanding when I became older. I didn't think I would.

That night I slept in the small waiting room, not wanting to spend the night in the hallway. Someone might not like it and complain, and they might take the sofa away. I didn't sleep much throughout the night. Around 3 a.m. I woke up and saw Dad standing by the doorway checking on me.

"Dad, is there anything wrong?"

"No, Mijo. Go back to sleep."

"Is Mom any better?"

"No, Arturo, the same. She is just sleeping. Just sleeping, Mijo. Go back to sleep." Dad appeared very sad and stressed. I didn't know if it was because there was no sign of Mom coming out of the coma or if it was because he was so tired. Dad was up for so many hours with her.

I went back to sleep for only a short time when I heard Uncle Ben say, "Arthur. Arthur, wake up!"

"Hey, Uncle Ben. What time is it?" I asked as I rubbed my eyes and pulled back my hair.

"It's early. Want to go eat with me?"

"Where is my dad?"

"He is sleeping in your mother's room. He'll be OK. The nurse said he didn't sleep all night and just now fell asleep. He won't even know you left. Come on."

"OK, Uncle Ben, I'll go."

In an hour we returned to the hospital. The day went slowly as we waited. During the afternoon family arrived again to see Mom. It was pretty similar to the day before, family coming and going.

The night was another sleepless one. Dad and I went at 3 a.m. to eat at the same restaurant where he told me the story about when he was shot.

Chapter Fifteen

Those Terrible Words

The following day started out much the same as the previous one with family who came and went. In the late afternoon the doctor went into Mom's room. Shortly thereafter, he came out and left. Uncle Ben stayed in Mom's room, sitting with her. Dad came out and sat with me on the sofa in the hallway; we were talking. Dad was filling me in on what the doctor had told him.

The door to Mom's room flew open. Uncle Ben dashed halfway out, holding the door open with one arm extended. "JOE! SHE'S WAKING UP!"

Dad jumped out of his sitting position and ran through the door and into the room. I also jumped up, feeling really happy. Dad and Uncle Ben raced to Mom's bedside. I stood by the door as it closed behind me, standing there observing my father and Uncle Ben next to my mother. Dad held Mom's hand. "Millie. Millie," Dad said with so much love in his voice. "Millie, can you hear me?"

Mom's hand was moving back and forth; her eyes opened a little. She looked around and then straight ahead as if she were in a trance. She wasn't coherent and was mumbling something. We were all waiting to see what she was going to say, feeling very happy Mom was coming out of the coma. We knew right then she wasn't going to die. I wanted to talk to Mom, but I knew if I said anything the nurse might have me leave. As a result I stayed where I was and remained silent.

Mom was moving her head slowly back and forth as if she wanted to say something. The dreadful words then came out, "Pete! Pete, where are you? Pete darling, honey."

Dad was shocked! He didn't understand what was happening and why Mom was calling out for another man. He opened his palms and raised his hands as if he was saying, "What?"

"Oh Peter. Peter," she expressed.

"What? Why? What is this? Who is Peter?" Dad took a step back, flabbergasted, and looked at Uncle Ben, asking, "What is wrong with her?" He thought she was going to be happy and pleased to see him next to her when she awakened He had no idea who she was asking for. Dad forgot the problems they were having, even sleeping in different bedrooms.

Uncle Ben had a very sad expression as if he really felt sorry for Dad. He lifted his shoulders and responded, "Joe, what can I say?"

"No! No! ¡No puede ser! (It cannot be!)" Dad was shocked. Mom's words related all the abuse she had taken from Dad through the years, as well as his relationship with other women. She had gotten tired of waiting for him and was lonely. She found someone new to take his place.

Dad stared at Uncle Ben as if he were wishing for him to say this wasn't true. "Benny! Benny! No!"

"I'm sorry, Joe. Maybe she is just delirious," Uncle Ben said knowing it was not true. My mother had confided in Uncle Ben already and he knew the real story.

Dad couldn't look at Mom. He turned his face. It looked as if he were going to explode right there in the room. I had never seen Dad look like this in all my life.

He turned around and saw me at the door. When he looked at me, I thought he was going to ask if, after all he shared with me, I knew how she really felt. If Dad had asked this of me, I would have answered, "I don't know anything," which was not true. Dad, however, should have known something as this might happen the way he had been leaving her and going out with other women. He appeared as if he was taking this pretty hard; he was a very proud man.

Dad started to walk in my direction and passed me, storming out of the room. He didn't say anything to me and acted as if I were invisible. Dad's face was red. I felt sorry for him with all of my heart. I thought of all we had talked about these past three days. It hurt to lose my father again. In this brief time I had a father; now it appeared he was gone again.

Uncle Ben stood there, not knowing what to say. Mom moaned a little more and went back to sleep. I stepped into the hallway feeling confused about the entire situation. "Why did Mom have to say that?" I asked myself.

In a little while Uncle Ben came out of the room. "Arthur, where is your father?"

"I don't know, Uncle Ben. I think he left."

"Shoot! That's too bad. I'll go and look for him. Maybe I can talk to him. I know he feels really bad. But you know, Arthur, he left your mother alone for too long. That's what happens when a husband leaves his wife alone."

"I'll go and look for your dad," Uncle Ben said as he walked away.

I didn't say anything; I was in shock. It was as if Mom told dad she loved someone else, despite the way he poured his heart out to me and expressed the changes he was going to make for her.

I stayed and waited for Uncle Ben. In two hours I went into Mom's room. She was starting to wake up.

"Mom, can you hear me?"

"Arthur. How are you?" Mom whispered as if she was waking from a deep sleep.

"I'm OK, Mom. I'm glad you are waking up. I was really worried about you."

Mom reached up and touched my face. "Where is your father?" she asked, closing her eyes as if she was going back to sleep.

"He was here, Mom; but he left. He's been here all this time. So has Uncle Ben. Uncle Ben should be back in a little while, Mom."

Just then Uncle Ben came in the door. "Millie, Sis! How are you feeling, Sis?" he asked, gripping his older sister's hand.

Mom nodded her head and didn't say anything else. She went back into a deep sleep.

The nurse stood from the chair where she had been sitting and stepped to where we were standing. She had watched the whole thing. "She will be waking up and going back to sleep as the hours pass; then she should fully recover. Hopefully in the next few days she will be wide awake," the nurse stated to us.

Dad had left and bought a bottle of whiskey. He couldn't believe things were turning out this way. He knew that Mom went out with

Sarah and her sisters, but he never imagined that she would fall in love with another man.

Dad's heart was deeply hurt. In the last three days, he had given thought to how he conducted himself with Mom throughout the years. He had made up his mind that he was going to make some big changes in his life for her. For the rest of his life, Mom was going to be the only woman for him. He had always loved her dearly but didn't show it the way he should have.

Dad drove his Cadillac around town, drinking his Ancient Age whiskey in straight gulps. He would think, "How could this be? My wife not wanting me by her side? ¡Ay, Millie! ¡AY, MILLIE, MI AMOR!"

Dad loved Mom so much, but he didn't show it as he should have. He really took her for granted those last few years, and now he knew it. For all we knew, she was just having a dream when she asked for another man. For that matter we didn't know if this is what she really meant because she was so groggy.

Dad drove to the hospital, parked his car, and thought he could take his bottle in with him as he sat by Mom's door to make sure she was all right. When he arrived at the hospital, he parked on 14th Street. Dad took his bottle out and took a big swallow.

Dad was in deep thought remembering how much he loved Mom; however, he could never go to her and beg. Not after she asked for someone else.

He took his bottle and gulped down another drink. From his rear-view mirror, he saw Uncle Ben running toward the car about a half a block away. Dad started up the car and pulled out of the parking space. He didn't want to talk to Uncle Ben. He felt he wasn't only losing his wife but her family as well. He now knew things could never be the same with them again. Dad was just too proud.

In his mirror he saw Uncle Ben stop running toward him. Uncle Ben waved, hoping Dad would see him and stop. Dad did see him. Regardless, in no way was he going to stop.

Dad drove around the hospital. When he reached 14th Street, Uncle Ben was gone. Dad saw his car parked, so he knew he was still in the hospital.

Inside, Uncle Ben walked down the hallway toward me. "Arthur, I saw your dad outside; but he left. What did he say? Did he talk to your mother?"

"No, Uncle Ben. He didn't come up here. Are you sure you saw him?"

"Oh yeah, it was him. He was getting in his car. When I started running toward him, he took off. I don't think he saw me. I thought he came up here. I wonder what he was doing?"

"I don't know. I wish he would have come up. I wanted to talk to him."

"And your mother? Has she woken up again?"

"Yeah, a few times. But she goes right back to sleep."

"I'm going to go and sit with her for a little while," Uncle Ben said.

After Uncle Ben went in to see Mom, I sat and thought about a lot of things Dad and I had discussed. I stood up and walked to the end of the hallway. When I approached the big window at the end of the hall, I stood and watched the traffic go by on Santa Clara Street. The sun was starting to set. I thought I saw Dad's Cadillac pass. "I know it's his car!" I thought. "But Uncle Ben said he left."

I stood there to see if Dad would drive by again. Within ten minutes he did. "Was he waiting for me to go out, so he could speak to me alone?" I asked myself. Hurriedly, I ran downstairs, almost falling, thinking I didn't want to miss him if he was waiting for me.

I exited the hospital through the front lobby on Santa Clara Street and looked around for his car. It wasn't parked anywhere. He slowly drove by again.

"Dad, over here!"

I started running toward him, but he kept driving, turning on 14th Street. I knew he would be back; therefore, I stood right on the curb so he could see me easier.

In about eight minutes he made his turn on 16th Street onto Santa Clara Street again. I stood facing him as he approached me. When he approached more closely, I raised my hand in order for him to spot me better. Dad pulled the car over, so the passenger window was in front of me. He was wearing his dark glasses; therefore, I couldn't see his eyes. He hit the "Push" button to lower the window on my side and said, "Arturo! How are you doing, Mijo?" Dad was speaking with his hard, strong voice. I could tell he had been drinking heavily.

"I'm OK, Dad. Are you all right?" I asked, bending over to see his face.

He didn't answer me but instead asked another question. "How is your mother?"

"She's getting better, Dad. She's coming out of it. She asked for you, Dad."

He took his fifth of whiskey and brought it up to his mouth, taking a big swallow. I continued, "Dad, Uncle Ben was looking for you. He wanted to talk to you."

Dad wiped the excess whiskey off his lips and said, "Take care of your mother, Arturo. Stay by her side. She is going to need you very much. Do you understand, Arturo?"

"Yes, Dad. I will. Are you going to come in?"

Dad put his hand on the window button and, as he stepped on the gas to pull away, he said, "Stay with her, Mijo!"

I stood and looked at the back of Dad's car. Tears came to my eyes. I wished Mom had never rejected him and asked for Pete. "Now look what happened!" I thought.

Standing on the curb for a few more minutes, I saw Dad come around the corner again. This time he didn't stop but kept driving to 14th Street. He made the turn again. I knew Dad was taking it really hard and didn't know what to think about the whole situation. I turned, proceeded back into the hospital, and walked up the stairs.

When I arrived at Mom's room, I stepped inside. Uncle Ben was sitting on a chair next to her. The nurse wasn't present.

"Did she wake up, Uncle Ben?"

"Yeah, she did. But just for a minute. It's all downhill now, Mijo. She will be OK now."

"Good. I'm so glad."

"The doctor just left. Do you know where your father went? The doctor wanted to speak to him."

"Dad is driving around the hospital in his car. He is driving around and around. I talked to him right now."

"Oh yeah? Is he coming back in?"

"No, Uncle Ben. I don't think so. He really looks sad. He's drinking whiskey. I think he really feels hurt in his heart. I told him Mom asked for him, but he didn't care."

"Yeah, Mijo. Some men really take this kind of thing hard. Your poor father. I'll go out and try to talk to him. Maybe he will listen to me," Uncle Ben stated.

I didn't say anything, choosing instead to sit and look at Mom. Uncle Ben stood up and placed his hand on my shoulder, saying, "I'll be back in a little bit." He walked out the door.

As I was sitting with Mom, Eddie came into the room. "How is Mom, Arthur?"

"Hi, Eddie. She's waking up."

Eddie stepped to Mom's side and held her hand. "Hi Mom! How are you?"

Mom lay there and didn't open her eyes. The area surrounding her eyes appeared very dark; I believe it was from the drug she had taken.

"Mom, can you hear me? Mom?"

Mom moved her head toward Eddie. She opened her eyes a little. "Hi, Mijo, Eddie. How are you, baby?" she whispered as she closed her eyes again. We didn't know if she went back to sleep or was awake with her eyes closed.

Eddie looked at me and asked, "Where's Dad, Arthur?"

"I think he's driving around the hospital. I talked to him a little while ago. Uncle Ben is here too, but he went outside to try to talk to Dad."

"Why is Dad driving around the hospital?"

I looked at Mom, stood, and motioned to Eddie to follow me into the hallway. We both went to the sofa, and I filled him in on what had transpired. Eddie felt very badly and shook his head. He didn't say much; he knew how Dad was and felt the same way I did about what happened. Eddie was hurt. He asked some questions, but I told him I didn't know the answers. All I knew was what I told him. We went back into Mom's room and sat with her. Eddie stayed with us.

In a little while Uncle Ben came back into the hospital room and joined us. I asked if he had spoken with my father. He answered, "Well, I tried; but he wouldn't talk to me. He didn't want to stop the car, and then he didn't come back around anymore. Your poor Dad. He is a good man. I wish the best for him. I hope he and your mother straighten this thing out. It's not good. I know! Look what happened to me and your tia (aunt)."

Later in the evening I was in the room alone with Mom. When

the doctor came in to see her, he remembered me. "Hello," he greeted. "Where is your father?"

"He's not here right now. But he'll be around later, Doctor."

He stepped to Mom's side, felt her pulse, picked up her chart, and read it. "Tell your father I need to speak to him right away. If he comes in, tell him to have me paged. I will be in the hospital for a few hours."

"OK, Doctor, I will."

"You do know that you are not supposed to be in here, don't you?"

"Yes, Doctor, but I hate to leave my mother alone."

"I know. All right. I think it will be all right. Let your father know I am expecting to hear from him. I think your mother will be fine now. I had the twenty-four-hour nurse watch discontinued because I do not feel there is any more danger to your mother."

"How long before all this stuff is out of her system?"

"That's what I wanted to talk to your father about. Tell him to page me."

"Thank you, Doctor. I'll tell my father as soon as I see him."

"OK, son. I will see your mother later," he said as he stepped out of the room.

During the rest of the day, Mom woke up a few times. I helped her drink water and spoke to her a bit. She was still very drowsy but was staying awake longer as the evening passed.

Later I went to the window and looked to see if I could see Dad drive by the hospital. It was dark outside. There was a lot of traffic on the street. In a few minutes I saw his Cadillac pass. I went out to the street again and waited for him. His good friend Ray was with him. He drove up to me once again and stopped. The window was already lowered. Ray greeted me; he too was wearing dark glasses. They both looked like gangsters in the car. Dad was fairly intoxicated by this time. "Mijo! How is your mother now?"

"She is a lot better, Dad. She wants to know where you are. She keeps asking for you."

Dad had his fifth of whiskey between his legs, "Stay with your mother, Arturo. Take care of her!"

"Dad, the doctor came by and said he needs to talk to you right away. He wants you to page him."

"OK, Arturo, I will call him. Have you seen your hermano Eddie?"

"Yeah, Dad. He was here and left a little while ago."

"Good! I will be out here, Arturo. If you need me, come out."

"Dad," I said, not sure what I wanted to say. I really wanted for him to forget what Mom said when she first woke up. I knew if he kept the plans of the things we talked about in the last few days, everything would work out fine. I just knew it would.

"What, Mijo?" Dad answered as if he knew what I was thinking.

"Dad, don't you want to come in?"

He had a very sad expression, but at the same time he looked as if he hated the whole world and life itself.

"No! I am not! You stay with her, Arturo! I will call the doctor later!" Dad stepped on the gas and drove away. His friend Ray put up his fingers and lifted his chin as if he were saying good-bye. It seemed as if he understood exactly how Dad felt.

I went back into the hospital and stayed with Mom for the following night and the next day. Dad called the doctor and was told that they really didn't know when all the drug would be out of her system. The doctor suspected it was not going to be long for Mom to fully recuperate. The doctor said she would have to stay in the hospital for a few days for observation. They wanted to make sure she was stable and would not become so depressed that she would take more pills.

Every day Dad would take us to see her; however, the two of them didn't speak. After two weeks Mom was released; we all went to pick her up at the hospital. All of us were really happy we were having our mom returned to our family. I know I really missed her at home. Things were just not the same without her. While she was gone, the house was quiet and gloomy.

The American Can Company was closing in four months. Dad was calling people and making arrangements to leave. In the weeks that followed, he didn't go out as much as he had in the past; however, he didn't speak to Mom. They both walked by each other without saying anything. It didn't seem that Mom cared if they spoke or not. When Dad wanted something from her, he would either tell us kids to tell her what he wanted; or he would speak to Mom in a harsh way. Things just were not right from that time forward.

I knew Dad really loved Mom, and the same applied to her. She loved Dad. It was just during this short period of time that she seemed not to care for him anymore. I knew these were her feelings because of the resentful way Mom stared at him when he wasn't looking at her.

Dad kept telling us he was leaving soon. The day finally arrived. He had all of his things packed to go, placed in suitcases and boxes tied with string. He embraced all of us, but not Mom. In an odd way I didn't want to see him leave; however, I felt once he left I would have it made. I would be able to do whatever I wanted. Mom would let me do a lot of things that Dad would have never approved.

During the months that followed Dad's leaving, Mom never spoke negatively of him. She didn't give us any reason to hate him as some women do. She told us we should always love him because we would never have another father who loved us as he did; he was our flesh and blood.

I really considered Mom's words about Dad and thought that I really didn't know if this was true. I remembered the fear I had of him when I was a child. When Dad left, I felt the worst thing in my life was now gone. No more would I have the fear of Dad coming home from work in a bad mood, looking for someone to be angry at. Although I had a good relationship with him during those few days at the hospital and felt I was able to see another side of him, I still felt relieved that he left.

Now Eddie, Tita, and I had free rein. Victor was still young. We went out with our friends and did whatever we wanted. Mom started going out to the clubs with her friends again. The following months were really wild.

Chapter Sixteen

The Turbulent Years

"Mom, can I borrow your car to go to the store?"

"No, Arthur. What if you get caught driving by the police or if you get in a wreck? Then what?"

"I won't, Mom. I'm just going to the Pink Elephant store. OK?"

"No. One of these days you're going to get caught with no license. You better not. I should have never let you go to the store the first time."

"But, Mom, you let me use your car yesterday. What's the difference between today and yesterday?" I knew if I bugged Mom long enough she would give in to me.

"All right, Mom? Let me use it. I'll be right back." I didn't need anything from the store, but I knew Mom would once she agreed to my request.

"OK, Arthur, but be careful! I don't want you to get into any trouble." Mom always gave in so easily. The times I drove her car, she really thought I was using it to go to the store.

After Dad left, she bought a clean, cool-looking, two-door, 1956 Chevy. It was white and light blue and had a three-speed transmission with the stick on the floor. Mom was happy that I was learning how to drive. She would have me go to the store for every little thing; no matter what, I never turned down her requests.

On one particular day I wasn't really planning on going to the store. I really wanted to go to my friend Bert's house and go cruising for awhile. Bert lived off White Road on Markingdon Avenue. We both were fifteen years old. Bert, Richard, and Frank were good friends. My other friend Ray, Phillip's cousin, lived in the same neighborhood as Bert.

I took the telephone, pulled the long cord outside of the house, and dialed Bert's phone number. "Hello. Is Bert there?"

Bert had a sister whom I liked, but no one knew it. She was really pretty. At the time, however, I had another girlfriend who lived not far from Bert's house.

"Is this Art?"

"Yeah. How are you? What are you doing?" It was Pat. I wanted to have a few words with her, thinking that if I had a car maybe she would want to go for a ride with my buddies and me.

"I'm fine. Are you calling for my brother?"

"Yeah, but. . ."

"OK. I'll get him. Hang on." Pat yelled out, "Bert, telephone!"

I was disappointed. When I went to Bert's house, she never gave me much attention. I always wondered if she noticed me because she sure didn't act as if she did.

"Yeah?" Bert answered. Bert was a thin, tall, dark guy with black, straight, short hair. He had a humorous personality, thinking everything was funny. Even when we were doing something bad, he would laugh and giggle. When we were drinking, he couldn't stop laughing. There was never a dull moment with Bert.

"Hey, man! What's up?"

"Hey, Art. Did you get the car?"

"Yeah, I did. I'll be right over, man."

"Cool!" Bert said happily.

"I told my mother I was going to the store. But when I get ready to leave, I'll ask her if I can go to your house too. I think I can talk her into it."

"OK, I'll be waiting for you. Try to hurry!"

"Hey, Bert, do you think Pat wants to go riding around with us?"

"My sister Pat? No way, man! I don't want her to go with us!" Bert laughed and then asked, "Are you crazy, Art? You want me to take my sister? Heck no, man!"

"OK, Bert. Hey, call Richard and tell him I'm coming. Tell Frank, too."

"OK, I will; but Frank won't go. Richard is waiting."

Frank lived next door to Bert. He had his own car, but his parents never let him go out with us. I felt they thought we were a bad influence on their son, which we were. Richard lived across the street from Bert.

"OK, I'll be over in a little while."

I hung up the telephone and put it back in the living room. Mom was in the kitchen.

"Mom, do you want me to get anything from the store for you?"

"Yes, Arthur. Get me a loaf of bread."

"OK, Mom. Do you have the money?"

"Yes. Get my purse."

I handed Mom her purse. As she was getting the money out, I asked, "Mom, can I stop at Bert's house? He wants me to go over to play ball with the guys there." I never played ball. I hated playing ball. I only did it in school because I had to play.

"I don't think so, Arthur. What if I want to use my car?"

"Just call me. I'll come right home. I'll stop playing and be here in no time."

"Well," Mom said hesitantly as she opened her coin purse.

"Please, Mom. It'll be OK. I'll be careful."

"OK, Mijo, but be careful! And come back with the bread first."

"All right, Mom. I will. Thank you, Mom," I said as I embraced her and gave her a kiss. My poor mother. She loved me so much that she believed everything I told her. She thought I was a really good kid.

I went out and started the car. I was too young to drive; however, one thing that helped was that I was tall for my age. When I drove, if I saw a cop, I would sit up straight to make myself look older.

I backed out of the driveway and drove slowly down Virginia Place, wishing to get the feel of the car before reaching King Road. I saw Fernando and Amador standing out in front of Fernando's house. Fernando squinted his eyes as he studied the car to see who was driving. Fernando had a light complexion and short, curly hair; he had very full lips.

As I approached them, I waved. Fernando waved at me and took a few steps out to the street to stop me. I stopped the car in the middle of the street. "Hey, Fernando. What's up?"

"Hey, man, your mother let you use her car? Where you going?" I could tell Fernando had been drinking. He was slurring his words. During this time the kids on Virginia Place sometimes started drinking early in the evening.

"First, I'm going to the store. Then I'm going to my friend Bert's house by White Road," I answered, trying to show off in front of him.

"Hey, we need a ride to my friend's house. Give us a ride."

"Where does he live?"

"By Capital Avenue."

"Sure. That's not far from where I'm going. Get in."

Fernando sat down on the front seat, and Amador stepped into the back seat. Richard flew out of the front door of his house and ran over to the car. "Where are you guys going?"

"Art is giving us a ride to Sam's house. Want to go?"

"Yeah, I'll go. How are we getting back?"

Fernando answered, "I don't know, man. We'll find a way. Let's go. Get in the back with Amador." Richard happily did so.

Fernando had a small bag with a can of beer inside of it. He brought it up to his mouth and took a drink. As he wiped his lips with his wrist, he said, "Let's go, Arthur. Let's see how good you can drive."

I drove down Virginia Place and made a right onto King Road, feeling a little nervous because I had never been cruising with these older guys in the car with me as the driver. I thought it was cool that I was driving around older guys. I turned down a side street to make my way through the back streets. It was safer to do this in order to keep out of sight of all the cop cars. We reached Capital Avenue and turned on the street where Fernando's friends lived. We parked, and Richard stepped out to ask for them. No one was home.

"Take us back, Art," Fernando insisted, slurring his words.

"OK, Fernando."

"Wait, Arthur! Stop!" he commanded.

Just as I pulled out in the street, I immediately pulled the car back over to the curb. Fernando stepped out and walked around to my side. He opened the door. "Move over. I'll drive."

I was caught by surprise and didn't know what to say, knowing I couldn't let him drive. My mother trusted me to go to the store for her, and now Fernando wanted to drive drunk. I had a lot of respect for him, but I didn't want him to drive. "What if something happens?" I thought.

"Come on, Art, move over!"

"Fernando, I'll drive. I don't think it'll be a good idea for you to drive. My Mom won't like it if something happens. If it does, she will never let me use the car again."

"Come on, man! You know nothing will happen! You've seen me drive a lot of times. Look how many rides I've given you when you have asked me."

Fernando was right. Sometimes he had his father's car or his uncles' cars. Whenever I needed a ride, he would never say no, even if it took him out of his way. Fernando was always all right with me. I sat there, debating if I should let him drive. I knew I shouldn't, but something told me I should remember all the good things he had done for me through the years.

"OK, Fernando, but be careful. Remember, it's my mom's car."

Fernando laughed as I got out and he moved behind the steering wheel. "Be careful? I'm always careful, Arthur! You know that!"

Richard, sitting in the back seat, agreed with Fernando. "He'll be all right, Arthur. He drives better drunk than when he's sober. And look how many times he has driven drunk and has never been in a wreck. He'll be OK. Don't worry, man!"

Amador didn't say anything. He was quiet. He didn't want to agree with me in front of Richard and Fernando, but he didn't want to end up going to Juvie for drinking and driving with someone.

We drove away. It seemed Fernando was driving fine; however, when I looked at his face, he looked as if he was concentrating really hard, staring at the road without moving his head. As he shifted gears, he didn't blink but kept his eyes wide open and focused. He wasn't relaxed at all. Every time he shifted the transmission, he released the clutch quickly and made the car jerk. It seemed as if he wasn't familiar with driving a stick shift. All the cars he drove, however- er were stick shifts; therefore, he did know how to drive them. Maybe it was the beer.

We made a turn onto Capital Avenue. A few blocks ahead was where we were going to turn right onto Bambi Lane, a residential street. A Ford station wagon was in front of us and was moving slowly. Fernando stepped on the gas as if he were going to hit the back of the Ford station wagon with the front of our car. He slammed on the brakes before hitting it, trying to get the driver to move faster. He wanted to let the diver know we were behind him. I watched how he was driving Mom's car and felt like telling him that he was damaging Mom's car by hitting the brakes as he was. I didn't say anything. He did it again and then a third time. His head was close to the steering wheel as he concentrated really hard on the car in front of us.

"Come on, idiot! Let's move it, man! We don't have all day!" Fernando snapped. He stepped on the gas again and tailed the car in front of us. It didn't appear as if the driver and passengers took any note of us behind them.

Fernando turned the steering wheel toward the gutter and stepped on the gas to pass the Ford station wagon on the right side. Just as our car was moving between the Ford station wagon and the gutter, the Ford's blinker flashed on our side. I was only able to see one blink as we pulled in rapidly. The Ford station wagon turned right into us as it started to make a right turn. This was why he was moving so slowly; he was getting ready to turn.

Boom! The car hit Mom's car toward the back as we were almost past it. I felt the car move and skid hard with the impact. My mind flashed back to thoughts of my mother. I knew she was going to be really angry.

"Man!" I shouted as I covered my face with one hand and held the dashboard with the other, just in case Fernando lost control of the car. I was really stressed about what I was going to do and disgusted with myself for letting Fernando talk me into allowing him to drive.

Fernando yelled out, "I got it! I got it!" He stepped on the gas and turned the steering wheel sharply to regain control. He also stepped on the gas to move away quickly. The car that hit us started to pull over. Fernando drove to the next corner and skidded around it hard. He stepped on the gas again and kept accelerating. "We have to get out of here! Don't worry, Art. I won't let them catch us!"

We kept moving down side streets and didn't stop or slow down. Once it seemed we were in the clear, I asked Fernando to pull over so that I could drive. I also wanted to check the damage that was done to Mom's car. "Fernando, pull over, man! Let me drive! Right here!"

"No, I got it! It's OK!" he yelled and reached for his beer, taking a big swallow. It appeared as if the can of beer was empty.

I was really worried and wondered what I was going to tell Mom. Her Chevy was really nice, and it didn't have one scratch on it when she bought it. Now what was I going to do? "Man!" I cried out and slapped the dashboard.

"Don't worry, Arthur, I'll get you home. The people didn't have time to get our license number. It's going to be all right, man! Trust me!"

"I'm not worried about that. I'm worried about what you did to my mom's car, man! What am I going to tell my mother?"

Fernando was still driving very fast. With one hand still on the dashbroad, I turned my body toward Fernando and yelled, "Hey, man, slow down now before you hit another car!"

Richard sat up in the back seat and asked his older brother, "Hey, Fernando, want me to drive? I'll drive. Pull over. Let me drive!"

Fernando laughed and said, "You're not going to drive me. Just hang on." Mom's car continued to move fast.

When we arrived on Virginia Place, we pulled over in front of Fernando's house. I grabbed the key as soon as he turned off the ignition and stepped out of the car to inspect the damage. "Man! Look at that!"

I kicked the tire and walked back and forth with my hands on my hips, not knowing how I was going to explain this to Mom.

As we were standing there, Donald, who lived a few houses down, came outside and walked to where I was standing. "Hey, what happened?"

"This," I said pointing to the dent.

"That's not that bad. You probably can just push that out. My uncle had a dent just like that. He went down under the back, reached up, and pushed the dent right out. And if that don't work, it'll be easy to fix."

"Think so?" I asked as I was starting to cool down. "Yeah, but what am I going to tell my mother?"

"Tell her? Why would you want to do that? Just leave it, and she'll think someone else did it. When you take the car home, drive it straight in the driveway so that she can't see this side. Later she'll think someone else did it."

"Good idea, man!" I said.

I now knew I had better go to the store right away, get the bread, and take the car back home before anything else happened. Before I left, Richard crawled under the car to see if he could push the dent out, but no such luck. It was damaged too much.

When I arrived home, I drove the car straight in the driveway so that when Mom came outside she wouldn't see the dent. I took the bread in the house. "Here is the bread, Mom."

"OK, Arthur. Thank you, Mijo. When are you going to be back from Bert's house? Nancy called, and I'm going out tonight. I'll need my car."

"Oh, Mom, that's all right. I don't have to use your car. I'll get a ride over there."

"Do you want me to drop you off, Mijo?"

I thought to myself, "If she drops me off, when she returns with the car, she might back it in as we normally do. She will surely see the damage."

"No, Mom, that's OK. Fernando has his uncle's car, and he said he would take me. But thank you anyway, Mom."

"Oh, Arthur, you are so good!"

Before leaving the house, I gave my mother a big kiss. As I kissed her, I felt bad that I wasn't being honest with her. I knew if I told her what really happened, I would never be able to use her car again and I didn't want this to be the consequence.

I left the house and started walking on the sidewalk, looking back at the car. "Man, I hope Mom doesn't see it before she leaves," I thought. I kept walking down Virginia Place.

When I passed Richard and Fernando's house, they came outside, concerned about what my mother had said about her car. They also wanted to know if I had told her that it was Fernando who wrecked it.

"No way, man! I would never tell her that. I'm the one who borrowed the car, and I'm the one who let you drive it. So it's my fault."

Richard asked, "What did she say about it?"

"I didn't tell her. I drove it straight in the driveway. The bad side was facing the other way, and the back end was close to the rose bushes. That way, when she leaves, she won't see it. Maybe she'll think someone else hit her in a parking lot or something. Man! I should have been more careful!"

Richard and Fernando felt sorry for me. As I started my walk to Bert's house, Fernando yelled out, "Hey, Arthur, do you want a ride? I'll get my uncle to come over and take you."

"No, that's all right. I can walk." I knew if Fernando's uncle came to get me it would be awhile before he arrived. "His uncle might not even show up," I thought.

It turned out that Mom went out and didn't see the dent. She thought someone at the nightclub hit her car in the parking lot. Nancy told Mom she thought she saw the dent when Mom picked her up, but she wasn't sure. My poor Mom had to pay to have her car fixed, costing her a lot. I felt really bad that I hurt Mom and that she didn't know I was the cause of her grief.

Years later, I told Mom the truth about the accident. Even though it was long after it happened, she was upset with me, labeling me "malcreado (disobedient)."

Chapter Seventeen

The Wild Guys

As time went by, Eddie and I became very wild guys, always fighting with other guys. I would hang out with my friends down the street and also go out with Eddie and his friends. It seemed as if some day we would end up in a fight, and someone was going to be hurt badly.

Eddie had something wrong with one of the tendons in his hand, requiring surgery. He was in the hospital for two days and then came home with his hand and wrist wrapped in a cast.

Rudy and Joe, who were brothers, came over to see if Eddie and I wanted to go out for the evening. I knew that if we went out and Eddie ended up in a fight I would have to back him all the way, even fight for him.

"Yeah, Rudy, we'll go out."

Eddie turned to me and asked, "What do you think, Art, want to go with us?"

"Yeah, I'll go. Where are we going?" I knew we always went to whatever party was taking place, but I thought maybe there was something special happening this time.

"I don't know," Rudy answered. "We'll find some good parties and pick up some nice looking girls."

This was something we always wanted to do whenever we had a chance, find girls and go cruising with them.

"Yeah, that will be cool. I'll take Lisa with me," Eddie said. Lisa was a girl Eddie liked a lot, a girl he dated on a steady basis. Lisa was a very pretty girl with long, brown, straight hair and a light complexion. She was slender and had a long, thin face.

"That sounds cool, Eddie," Rudy said. "I'll be back around 8 o'clock to pick you guys up."

"We can go in my car," Eddie replied. He had bought a two-door, 1953 Chevy. It was dark brown with a light brown top, lowered, and had chrome rims.

"Yeah, whatever. I'll see who else wants to go, and maybe we'll take both cars." Rudy said. He had a red, lowered, 1963 Red Chevy Impala, really cool looking. Both of them wanted to take their nice looking cars.

Later that night Rudy came to the house, and we left. First we picked up Lisa. Next we drove to Joe and Rudy's house to pick up Joe, his brother. Leo would also be there because Leo was Joe's shadow, always with him. We all put in money and bought two cases of beer.

Parked at Donald's house and drinking beer, we were approached by Richard and Fernando. Fernando stepped into Rudy's car, and Richard got into Eddie' car. Conrad, who lived two blocks down the street, came over to join the rest of us.

Fernando, sitting in the back seat of Rudy's Impala, said, "Hey, let's go to Wesley's party."

"Is he having one tonight?" Rudy asked.

"Yeah, that's what I heard."

"Man, that guy has cool parties," Rudy added.

"Let's go, man!" I said, already feeling high from the beer. Wesley was an African American guy who threw big parties.

Donald was sitting shotgun. The two cars were backed in the driveway, side-by-side. Eddie was in the driver's seat of his car. Donald turned to Eddie and asked, "Hey, Eddie, want to go to a party, man?"

"Whose party? Where?"

"Fernando said Wesley is having a party tonight. Want to go?"

Eddie turned and looked at Lisa. Lisa had an expression which seemed to say she wanted to go as well. Lisa really liked dancing and having fun.

Eddie turned back and replied, "Sure, let's go. What time is it?"

"What time is it, Art?" Donald asked as if I had a watch.

"I don't know, man. I know it's not that late."

"Anyone know?" Donald asked everyone. On the street in front of us a car passed by slowly as if he, the person inside, was looking for someone. It was dark, and they couldn't see us in the cars.

Eddie said, "Hey, man, let's wait for a little while and drink a few beers before going. We don't want to be the first ones there."

Leo said he heard there was a party on the north side behind the Northside Market. We decided to take a ride to that part of the city to check it out personally. Sometimes if parties didn't look that good, we would just drive by a few times and leave.

We drove in the Impala with Rudy, Donald, Fernando, Conrad, and me. Eddie, Lisa, Richard, Leo, and Joe were in Eddie's car. The car I was in took the lead; Eddie followed us. It was a little difficult for Eddie to drive with his cast; he had a three speed on the steering column.

There were a lot of people standing around in the front yard of the party. It was dark, although there was one street light in front of the house. The house was an older, Victorian home with a nice front yard. It had grass, some rose bushes, and other plants next to the driveway. The party was in a rear house at the end of a long driveway.

We decided to leave our cars and check out the party. We parked, and Eddie parked a few houses away. When we stepped out of our cars, we all came together and started walking toward the house. As we were walking, some of the people turned to see if they knew who we were.

We saw Johnny Martinez with his friends. It was just a few weeks before that Fernando was in a fight with Johnny. They both had danced around in that fight, and no one really won. Johnny had about thirty guys after school with him; and Fernando had about fifteen, including me. Now Richard, Fernando's younger brother, wanted to fight Johnny. Richard was a much better fighter than Fernando.

As we approached the long driveway, Johnny was with a few of his friends, walking toward the back of the driveway. Richard yelled out, "HEY, MAN!"

Johnny turned around and saw who was yelling. He appeared worried. He didn't want to fight Richard because he knew he might lose. Just then all the guys at the back of the driveway came together. There were about twenty of them. It was their party. Richard asked us, "You guys ready, man?"

I really didn't care how many guys Johnny had with him; I was confident we could handle them. I knew Eddie couldn't fight well because of his hand injury. It was only the rest of us, but we were all good fighters. It didn't matter if we were outnumbered; I felt like fighting.

One of the guys with Johnny yelled out, "Hey, man, if you guys are going to be here, we don't want any pleito (fight)!"

Johnny didn't say anything. It appeared as if he didn't want any trouble either. As we approached them, Richard spoke up; the rest of us waited for Richard to take the first swing. When that happened, we knew it was time to jump in, especially with the beer we had already drank.

"Hey, John, you fought my brother the other day; and now it's my turn to kick your behind, man!"

"Not here, Richard. This is my friend's party; and I don't want to mess things up, man."

Richard stood there for a minute and thought about what Johnny said. He thought that if it was so then it wouldn't be a good time to fight him. Also, if he were telling the truth, this meant everybody there at the party was on Johnny's side. It would, therefore, not be a good time for us either.

"OK, man, there'll be another time. I'll be looking for you, man!"

I stood there and gave Johnny's friends a hard stare, wanting to fight someone. If one of the guys would have said anything, I was planning on hitting him as hard as I could.

Richard turned around and said, "OK, let's go. The sissy don't want to fight because he doesn't want to mess up his friend's party, probably another sissy!"

We all turned around and walked away. Johnny and his friends had a reputation of being tough guys also. When they fought someone, it was never one-and-one. Johnny and his friends always had to jump into a fight. We knew this and were expecting it. We were ready for it.

We all returned to our cars and drove away. I turned my head as we were leaving and saw two guys in front who earlier were in the back of the driveway with Johnny. They were making sure we left.

Donald said, "OK, let's go to Wesley's party now. I think it's going to be a lot better than this one!"

We all had a beer as we were cruising. When we arrived at the east side, we drove to Wesley's house. There was no parking available because there were a lot of people at the party. Even in the street we had to creep along in the car because of all the people who were standing around talking.

The homes were tract houses that were about three or four years old. The neighborhood was clean and kept up nicely.

We drove around the corner, parked, and stepped out of the cars. Richard asked if anyone wanted to take an extra beer just in case they didn't have any at the party. Some of the guys took one extra bottle of beer and put it in their pockets. Rudy and Joe drank what they had left in their bottles and took two beers each with them. One beer they opened, and the other they put in their pockets. I still had half of mine; therefore, I was all right with one extra beer. I didn't want to walk back to the car for another bottle.

From where we were, we could hear the band playing cool oldies around the corner. We all started our walk toward the party. Some girls we knew said hello to us as we were walking toward the house. People would turn and look to see if they recognized us as we walked by them. Some of them we had seen around at other parties, but I didn't know them personally. They were much older than I was.

Once we arrived, we went into the house. There was standing-room only. As soon as I entered the house, I recognized the band, specifically one of the band members who played the guitar. His name was Roy. Roy was an all right guy and was always playing at parties with his band. We knew each other from gatherings around town and with other friends.

Eddie and Lisa found a seat on the sofa. I stayed standing on the side next to them. The rest of our friends were scattered all around the house. Inside the house it was dark. People were dancing all over the living room floor. All I could see were heads and bodies bobbing up and down with the music. It was very crowded. There were a lot of girls as well as guys in the house. Outside the front door there was also standing-room only. I stood by the sofa drinking my beer. In just a few minutes, I finished the beer and took out the extra one I brought from the car, putting the empty bottle next to the sofa on the floor.

I had not seen Wesley, although I really didn't know him. For that matter he didn't know me. Eddie, Richard, and Fernando knew him well. I really didn't know anyone at the party, only the band member Roy. They were all older people.

Eddie wasn't a good dancer and didn't dance much, although he would after a few beers. I was the same. Some guy came to the sofa and said, "Lisa, hey baby, how are you?"

Lisa smiled flirtatiously and said she was fine and came to have fun.

The guy asked, speaking loudly because it was so noisy, "Hey, Lisa, want to dance?"

Lisa didn't understand what he said. "What?"

"WANT TO DANCE?" he asked again and pointed to the dance floor.

"Sure!" Lisa answered, standing up and reaching for the guy's hand.

I looked at Eddie; he didn't seem too pleased. As Lisa and the guy were dancing, I saw him saying something in her ear. She looked at him, smiling and batting her eyes. The number was over, and a slow dance followed. They came together and were dancing very close and slow. I looked down at Eddie again, still sitting on the sofa; he was getting more upset as he watched Lisa and the guy. I wanted to walk away and look for someone to dance with, but I figured that it was best to stay there, just in case Eddie really became angry and wanted to fight with the guy. I knew I would have to back him up because his hand was in a cast.

In a few minutes the dance was over, and Lisa started to make her way toward us. The guy was right behind her. Just as she was going to sit down next to Eddie, the guy grabbed her by the arm and pulled her back to dance again. Lisa smiled at him and followed him back onto the dance floor.

Eddie didn't like it one bit. He stood up. As they came together to dance, Eddie stepped to the middle of the dance floor. "Hey, Lisa! Come on! Let's go and sit down." Eddie was upset because she had arrived with him, and now she was dancing every dance with this guy. Lisa was explaining to Eddie that it was just dancing, and there was nothing wrong with it. The guy stood there watching. I didn't want to take any chances with his taking a swing at Eddie, so I moved close to them.

Eddie said, "Come on, Lisa, let's sit down or leave."

"Hey, ese, why don't you sit down!" the guy told Eddie in fighting words. Eddie took a step back and let go with a hard punch. The other guy was ready to come back with his own punch when I reached back, let my beer bottle drop to the floor, and moved forward, releasing my punch. My punch landed right on the guy's face. He didn't know what hit him and went tumbling back, falling to the floor.

Someone pushed me. I hit him as well. He threw his beer bottle at me and missed. The person the bottle had struck yelled. Someone there ran next to me in a jumping mode to get the guy who threw the bottle.

There was someone else swinging next to Eddie, so I started fighting with him. As I was swinging, I noticed that everyone in the house was fighting. It was a free-for-all, just like fights in a saloon in the old cowboy movies.

Even though the fight was really getting wild, the band kept right on playing. I looked at my friend Roy; he ducked as a beer bottle flew by him. It didn't stop him from playing his guitar. He was used to playing at wild parties like this one.

People were shouting and swinging. I lost sight of Eddie, but I knew he was swinging somewhere in the house.

Everyone was pushing toward the front door. People wanted to go outside because there was more room to fight. I felt as if I were in a football game and was being pushed out the front door by a mob. As everyone was moving out the door, many tumbled down to the ground and over the step of the front porch. As I made my way outside, the fight started to cool down even more.

All the guys who were out front were older, mean looking guys. I felt small next to them. Donald and Leo were already outside. We made our way to the sidewalk. In the house people were still yelling. Guys were standing by the front door with blood on their faces and clothes. I saw Eddie and Lisa walking toward us with Richard and Fernando behind them. Just as they approached, a really big, heavy guy named Danny came crashing out of the house, yelling, "Who started this?" He was walking through all the people with his big body swinging from side-to-side, really upset. His head moved back and forth as if someone was going to say, "I did!" He had a mob of big guys behind him with torn and bloody shirts. It appeared as if he found the person who started it; they were all going to beat the heck out of him. He yelled again, "Who started this?"

I didn't say anything. I sure wasn't going to volunteer any information and commit suicide! As the mean looking guy approached us, Eddie's eyes gave me a look as if he were saying, "Shh, don't say anything."

I wasn't about to say anything. Fifteen guys surrounded us. Danny, the big guy, looked at Fernando and asked, "Hey, Fernando, they said it was one of your guys who started the fight. Who was it? I want that guy!"

Fernando really didn't know who started it. He wasn't near us when Eddie and I took the first swing. He said, "Hey, man, I don't know. If it were one of us, I would tell you so that you and I could get down right now! But it wasn't."

Fernando and Danny were about the same age. Danny didn't say anything. He wasn't sure he wanted to fight Fernando because then he would be an enemy with our group of guys and would stay that way for a long time.

"Man!" Danny yelled, still really angry. "If I find out who it was, I'm going to get him myself! It's going to be him and me!" His eyes stopped on me as if he knew I was the one who started the fight.

I laughed to myself even though I was a little worried, thinking, "Man, if I have to fight this big guy alone, I'm going to have a hard time putting him down!" I knew if it came to that we all were going to have a hard time fighting them. I wasn't going to fight alone; my brother and our friends would back me up in a second. I didn't say one word and waited to see what was going to happen, looking around for the guy I hit. I didn't see him.

Richard said, "Let's go. Let's go to another party." Richard was the kind of guy who, if Danny had told him anything, Danny was going to have a fight on his hands if he liked it or not. Danny was probably going to lose it too!

Richard turned and started to walk toward the cars. We all followed him and left the other guys standing there with his friends.

When we arrived at our cars, we were laughing. For those who didn't know, they were told that Eddie and I were the ones who started the whole thing. Fernando looked at me and said, "Man, Art, if I would have known that, I would have told Danny you were the one!

Then we could have kept right on fighting!"

As the months went by, we did end up in big trouble. Eddie and I were sent to the California Youth Authority, the prison system for young offenders. We were locked up for three years because of fighting. Mom went to see us only a few times. She worried very much for both of us. I was in an institution closer to home, Preston. Eddie was in Southern California, Y.T.S. Mom said she couldn't afford to visit Eddie. She felt that if she couldn't see him then she couldn't come to visit me either. She felt this was the only fair way to treat both of us.

In Preston, Tita wrote me letters letting me know what was going on at home. She told me Mom was going out a lot. She also told me Mom worried very much about Eddie and me. Before I was released, she said Mom had a boyfriend who lived in the house. Mildred or Tita as we called her, didn't like Mom's boyfriend at all.

The day I arrived home from Preston, I met Mom's boyfriend and didn't like him very much either. He was the kind of man who drank and cried for Mom to forgive him for everything.

Eddie was released a month earlier than I was. He already had a job working at a chrome plating shop. When I got out, I found different low-paying jobs. When I came home, I didn't hear from Dad for a long time.

I later married Tina and moved to Long Beach, California. When I was twenty-one, I found a job at American Can Company in Wilmington, California. A supervisor at the company knew my father well from the American Can Company in San José. Douglas always spoke well of my father.

During this time I saw my father a few times when he would come to Los Angeles. Dad married a young girl in Mexico who was only two years older than I was. Angelita's parents lived in San Gabriel, California, in the Los Angeles area. She was the youngest of her 23 brothers and sisters. Her family liked my father very much, even though he was much older than she was.

I rented a small, but very nice, one-bedroom apartment ten blocks from the beach. Outside of the apartment units was a lot of greenery, making the housing appear as if it were a resort.

The owner of the building liked me very much and asked if I wanted to be the manager of the apartments. I told him I would. I asked what the pay and benefits would be. There were only 12 units;

and all I had to do was collect the rent from everybody, making sure there wasn't any trouble. If there was, I was to call the owner on the telephone; he would be right over to handle the situation. In return, he deducted half my rent.

It was so nice living there that sometimes I would walk to the beach with a five-gallon bucket, going over to the big rocks and reaching down to the water, pulling out big crabs. I placed them in a bucket and took them home to have a crab meal. I really enjoyed living in Long Beach.

Tina was having our first baby. I couldn't believe I was going to be a father to a child. It seemed unreal to me.

The second the baby arrived, I was very proud. When I left the hospital, I bought two boxes of cigars and was passing them out to everyone, even people I didn't know. As I gave out the cigars, I said, "It's a boy!"

Chapter Eighteen

Making Peace

From the hospital I called my mother and told her the good news. I also called other relatives and let them know about the new addition to the family, including calling San Gabriel to see if my father had arrived. I knew he would be in town soon because the last time he was there, four months previously, Dad said he wanted to visit us to see his first grandchild.

My father changed a lot from the way I knew him when I was a kid. Now that I was grown, he was a different man. The last few times I saw him in the Los Angeles area, he seemed like the father I grew to know at the hospital when my mother was ill.

"Hello, this is Art, José's son. Is my father there?" It was my father's father-in-law.

"No, Arturo, he is not here; but we are expecting them anytime soon. They called last week and told us they would be arriving sometime during the week."

"OK, thank you. Tell him my son has been born and that everything went well. I just wanted to let him know."

"OK, muchacho (boy). I will tell him as soon as he gets in."

Tina and our new baby were coming home the next day at about 2 p.m. Just as I was going to leave the house to pick them up at the hospital, the phone rang. "Hello."

"Arturo! Hey! Congratulations, Mijo! I am so proud to be a grandfather," my father said in his strong voice. I sensed that he was already drinking.

"Hi, Dad! It's a boy!"

"I know, Arturo. Everything went good?" he asked.

"Yeah, everything went well. I'm leaving right now to bring them home from the hospital. I'll be back in about an hour or two."
"OK, Mijo, I'll be over right now. I'm taking a taxi to Long Beach. Give me the address again."
"All right, Dad. It's 1036 Chestnut Street."
"OK, Mijo. I'm coming! Keep the baby awake, so I can see who he looks like!" Dad said with his powerful laugh.

I hung up the telephone and left to the hospital.

At the hospital, on the way down the elevator, I held my new baby in my arms. The feeling was strange. I didn't think I was capable of creating another life and still couldn't believe the little baby I was holding was really mine. He was little and cute, with a round, swollen face. I thought he looked just like me!

Once we were outside, the nurse opened the door for my wife to step out of the wheelchair and step into the car. My wife prepared to hold our son as I started to hand him to her. I didn't want to release our baby. I wanted to hold him and drive at the same time.

"Come on, let me have him," Tina insisted.

"OK, OK," I said as I reached in and handed him to her. It felt as if his tiny body could fit in the palm of my big hand. Now that I had become a man, I had very large hands, bigger than the average person. I stepped into the other side of the car and drove home.

Once we were home, we took the baby into our one-bedroom apartment. Besides the one bedroom we had an average-sized living room. We didn't have a lot of things, only a couch and a chair, end tables with lamps, and a coffee table. On the wall we had a picture of a ship painted on felt. I bought it in Tijuana, Mexico, for $10 a few months earlier.

Just as I closed the door, the phone rang; I picked it up. "Hello," I answered.

"Mijo, hi!"
"Hi, Mom!"
"How is the baby, Arthur?" Mom asked excitedly.
"He is so little, Mom. Was I that little when I was born?"
"You weighed 7 pounds 4 ounces. How much did your baby weigh?"
"He weighed 7 pounds and 2 ounces. Man, I can't believe I was that little. But, Mom, my baby is really cute!"

Mom thought I was funny and laughed. She replied, "I know, Arturito. Isn't it a good feeling? I remember when all my babies were born; it always feels the same. I am so happy for you."

"Thank you, Mom."

"Listen, Arthur, I'm leaving our airport tomorrow about 11 in the morning. Can you pick me up at the airport at noon?" To drive to Los Angeles from San José took eight hours. A plane only took forty-five minutes.

"Sure, Mom," I answered. Once I answered, I remembered my father was also coming to visit. My mother and father had never really spoken to each other since the divorce.

I didn't know what to say. I couldn't tell Mom not to plan her visit, and I couldn't call my father and tell him the same. He was already on his way. I wondered if I should tell Mom he was also arriving to visit. Maybe if I told her, she would think of something for me. I thought, "No, I won't say anything. It's not my fault they had all those problems back then. I'll just wait to see what happens. Maybe Dad is just coming for the day. Then I won't have anything to worry about when Mom arrives."

"OK, Arthur, I'll see you then. Do you need anything? Do you want me to bring anything for the baby?"

During this time my job paid well. I had bought what we needed and also received other items from a baby shower that friends and family hosted for us. We had been buying necessities for the baby for the last few months, and the crib was filled with receiving blankets and baby clothes.

"No, Mom. I think we have everything. But if there is anything you would like to get for the baby, you can."

"All right, Mijo. I'll see you when I arrive at the airport tomorrow."

"OK, Mom, I'll see you then."

"Bye," Mom said.

"Bye, Mom." I hung up the phone, wondering what was going to happen if she arrived and my father was still with us.

We had been sitting on the sofa admiring our new son. In a little while there was a knock on the door of the apartment. When I opened the door, I found it was Eddie, Uncle Ray, and Aunt Connie.

"Hey! Come in!"

Uncle Ray and Aunt Connie lived in the small city next to Long Beach, a city named Wilmington. It was about 11 miles away. In the Los Angeles area, all the small cities are connected together. Eddie lived in San José but came to visit for a few weeks. He was twenty-two, a single guy, and wasn't tied down to a job or a family.

My aunt gave me a hug. She was the same age as Eddie and was my mother's youngest sister. Her husband Ray was really a cool uncle. He was a good guy with my brothers and sister. "Where's your baby, Arthur?"

"Right there, Aunt Connie," I said, pointing to the little cradle in front of the sofa.

"Let me see!" she said. Her two little girls, Rita and Nancy, followed her to the baby. I knew they were going to want to hold our son and was worried the baby might contact germs. I knew the other family members who lived nearby were going to also come and visit. I even thought of going to the store to buy some facemasks because I didn't want the kids to spread germs on our new son. I didn't want him to get sick.

"Hey, Art, what's up? New baby, huh? You made me an uncle!" Eddie said.

"Yeah, you're an uncle now! You're turning into an old man!"

"Man, Art, you're making me old!"

Eddie had no interest in getting married as of yet. He liked his single life. He would go to Mexico on trips for months at a time. In addition, he had not found the girl with whom he wished to spend the rest of his life.

Eddie stepped over to the baby as Aunt Connie picked him up and took him from the cradle.

"What a cute baby! Look, Ray, he looks just like Art!"

"Let's see that baby!" Uncle Ray said.

Aunt Connie faced our son toward her husband. I wanted to reach and take him away from her. It appeared as if his head was going to fall off his shoulders. She wasn't mishandling the baby, but I was being a little over protective as a new father.

Uncle Ray asked, "Is he going to be a Rams fan? If he is, then I'll say he's cute. If not, then I don't know!" We all laughed.

"Eddie, Dad is coming over right now."

"He is? Right now? Did you talk to him?"

"Yeah, he called a little while ago and said he was taking a taxi to come here."

"Good, I'll see him too," replied Eddie.

"But that isn't all. I don't know if he is going to spend the night. Mom called right now and said she is going to be on a plane at 11 in the morning. She's coming here too. She asked if I could pick her up from the airport. So that means they'll both be here at the same time."

"Wow," Eddie said, thinking the same thing I was when I finished my call with Mom. "What do you think is going to happen?"

"Man, I don't know. I don't know what to do. I was going to tell Mom that Dad is coming, but I didn't. I thought it wasn't my fault they divorced because of everything that happened."

"Yeah, you're right. It's not a situation we created."

"Hey, Eddie, want to spend the night? That way you can be here with me when Mom gets here. I don't want to be alone if there's a big fight between them and I end up needing help to calm them down. Just tonight. If they don't have a big fight when she gets here, then I think it'll be all right."

"Sure, I'll spend tonight here; and I'll be here when Mom gets here."

Eddie had been spending his time at Uncle Ray and Aunt Connie's. Before I was married, I spent time there also. They were really cool to be around, always making things fun.

"OK, that will be cool. I can use anything you can give of your time. Man, I don't know what to tell Mom on the way home from the airport."

"Just tell her, Art. What can she say? You didn't plan it this way, so don't worry about it. Just tell her that Dad came to see the baby too, and he is at your apartment."

"Yeah, you're right. That's what I'll do, just tell her like that."

In a little while Eddie decided he was going to take Uncle Ray and Aunt Connie back to Wilmington and return to our apartment to see Dad.

A half-hour after Eddie left, there was a knock at the door. I opened it to find a taxi man. "Excuse me, but I'm looking for an Arthur Rodriguez. I have a man in the car who wants me to see if his son lives here before he gets off."

"Yeah, I'm Art. That's my father," I said as I stepped out the door, heading to where my father was sitting.

When Dad saw me, he opened the door and stepped out of the back seat. "¡Arturito! ¡Mijo! I found you! Good!" he said as he embraced me.

"Good to see you, Dad."

"I want to see the baby," Dad said as he turned to the taxi man, asking him to get his suitcase and to take it into the apartment. Dad was accustomed to giving orders to people. He was now a businessman and owned a pharmacy where he bought and sold many items for a profit. He felt he was very important.

Once he stepped into the house, he saw the baby and laughed happily, knowing my son was the first of many grandchildren. He made the taxi man wait a few minutes while he said his hellos. The taxi man didn't seem to mind. On the drive to my house, Dad had made friends with him, one of his many talents. Dad took out a large bill and paid him, telling him to keep the change. I didn't see how much it was, but the taxi man appeared very pleased.

We sat in the living room and talked. Dad asked if we could open the door because it was very warm in the apartment. I felt it should be hot because the baby was accustomed to being in his mother and it was 98 degrees inside her body.

"No, Dad, I have to keep it warm for the baby. I don't want him to get sick." That was the first time in my life I had ever turned down a request from my father.

"No, Arturo, he is not in his mother anymore. He is out here like us. It will be OK. I know, I was a father to four of you."

"No, I don't think so," I said, looking down at our new little baby. I was determined to do everything I could to make life nice for him. "It needs to stay warm in here."

My father didn't say anything more about the temperature of the apartment. I knew he wanted to, but he didn't.

Dad asked for a glass. He took out a bottle of whiskey from his suitcase and poured some into the glass. Eddie came back from dropping off my uncle and aunt. We all talked and drank some tequila that Dad brought for us. I eventually went to a nearby fast food restaurant and picked up something for dinner.

That night Eddie and Dad slept in the living room, Dad on the couch, Eddie on the floor.

In the middle of the night, I heard the front door open but didn't hear it close. I stepped out of bed, opened my bedroom door, and looked into the living room, standing there and trying to make out what was in the dark. It was Dad. He had the front door open and was bent over with his head leaning outside. All he was wearing was his white undershorts. I heard him say, "Mijo, Eddie! Come on, let's go to a motel! Don't worry, I'll pay! I can't take this heat!"

"I don't know, Dad. Arthur wants us to be here. If we suffer just for the one night, it'll make him feel good."

I spoke up, "Dad, what are you doing? Close the door! The baby is going to get sick!" The baby was in our bedroom, and I had the door closed. He was all right, but I didn't want to take any chances.

"Mijo, you have it too hot in here! You are going to kill us!"

I knew I wasn't going to kill them. I just didn't want Dad to kill our little baby with the cool air! It wasn't really that cold outside, maybe about 65 degrees. Dad finally closed the door when I agreed to turn the heater down a little. The rest of the night went well.

The next morning also went well. We were having breakfast when I told Dad that Mom was going to be arriving at noon. I was really nervous about what he was going to say, remembering back to when I was young. They had not spoken to each other for a couple of months before Dad left back to Mexico.

"Dad, Mom is coming. I have to pick her up at the airport at noon." Los Angeles Airport was about a forty-five minute drive, one-way, from my apartment.

"She wants to come to see the baby and will be staying here too."

I didn't know where everyone was going to sleep. It was just a small, one-bedroom apartment. They would have to sleep in the living room, unless Dad decided to go to a motel or to return to San Gabriel, which was about an hour's drive.

"Good! I haven't seen your mother for a long time. It will be good to see her again."

"Oh, well," I thought. That was easy.

At noon I was at the airport waiting for Mom to arrive. I only waited for fifteen minutes when I saw her through the glass door. She looked really nice. It was good to see her. I loved Mom so much. I stepped out of my car and went to help her with her suitcase. "Hi,

Mom! How are you?" I said as I embraced her.

"I'm fine, Arturito. How is Tina and the baby?"

"They're fine, Mom. I can't wait till you see the baby. You'll love him so much."

Mom laughed as I opened the trunk of my blue, 1956 Buick Special and put her baggage in it. She said, "I already love him, Arthur. He is my first grandchild."

I walked around and opened Mom's door. Once she was in, I shut the door and ran to the other side, hopping inside as well. I drove away from the passenger pick-up zone.

"Mom, I want you to know that Dad is at my apartment too. He came to see the baby and spent the night. I don't know if he is going to spend the night again," I explained, worried, not knowing if Mom was going to accept this.

She didn't say anything for a minute. I didn't know if she was going to be angry or if she didn't mind. Through the years she never spoke badly about Dad. She didn't make us hate him. "That's OK, Arthur, I haven't seen him for a few years. It will be nice to see him again."

Mom used to love Dad very much. I thought that perhaps such deep love never goes away. Maybe Mom still had feelings for Dad, even though she had other boyfriends through the years. Dad was even re-married, but I wondered if Dad still had the same feelings for her.

Again, I was nervous when we arrived at my small apartment. I thought to myself, "Well, at least we'll eat better than we did yesterday. With Mom here, she'll cook for us."

As we were walking down the walkway on the side of the apartment building, I could tell Mom was also nervous. The garden at the side of the building to my apartment was very pretty. It had many large plants and resembled a small jungle. Mom wasn't saying anything. All she said was, "You live in a nice place, Arthur."

"Thank you, Mom. It's a little far from work, but I like it here. I'm close to the beach. Sometimes I walk down there and catch my own crabs."

She didn't answer, probably thinking about what might take place with Dad. I opened the door for Mom to enter first. Eddie and Dad were already on their feet. Dad had taken a shower to look good for

Mom. As soon as we stepped in, I smelled Dad's cologne. Eddie hugged Mom and asked if she was following him. They both laughed.

Mom said, "Yeah, sure!"

Dad was standing behind Eddie to take his turn to greet Mom.

She looked at Dad, and he said, "¿Millie, como estas (how are you)?"

"Joe, it's good to see you. You look very good, as handsome as always," Mom said with a very affectionate smile.

Dad reached to embrace her. She returned his tight squeeze. It seemed as if they never wanted to release each other. They stood holding each other; it appeared as if they never wanted for that moment to end. I didn't want it to end either. Eddie and I stood there, not saying anything. We waited quietly until it was over. I wished Mom and Dad would fall in love again and that it would never end. Maybe they still loved each other after all these years.

Finally they separated from their long embrace, telling each other they missed one another. We all sat down while Mom went to the bedroom with Tina to see the baby. I hoped things would go well during the entire visit; however, I knew how Dad's personality could change very quickly when he was drinking. I also knew Mom was very independent now and that she wasn't going to let him tell her what she could and couldn't say or do. When we were kids, Dad would order Mom around; she would do whatever he demanded.

Mom returned to the living room and sat down. For the next few hours, we all talked. Mom and Dad spoke but were very reserved, not wanting to get too close to one another. There were still a lot of bad feelings.

Mom went into the kitchen to see what she was going to make for dinner. She asked me to go to the store to buy some items. Dad asked me to buy him a bottle of whiskey, cigarettes, and some beer for Eddie and me. I left and returned in a little while.

Dad started drinking his hard liquor. Eddie and I drank beer and talked. I put on some music to try to ease the tension that was in the air with Mom and Dad. During the afternoon and evening, other relatives came by to see the baby, including my grandmother.

My grandmother and grandfather lived in the same apartment building that Uncle Ray and Aunt Connie rented, with Uncle Joe, my mother's youngest brother, and Aunt Linda living in a triplex behind them. They all moved to Wilmington some years ago; Uncle Ray was from Wilmington.

After dinner was over, Mom cleaned the kitchen very quickly. Later that evening she had a couple of beers. As the evening progressed, Mom and Dad experienced a few small confrontations, nothing major. Dad wasn't pleased that she didn't agree with him on some matters. Mom now spoke her mind, and she didn't care what Dad thought. She was going to speak up; if he didn't like it, it was just too bad.

As the evening grew late, I found myself feeling really tired. Eddie left to stay at Uncle Ray and Aunt Connie's apartment. I told Mom and Dad I was tired, telling Dad he could sleep on the floor and Mom on the sofa. They felt this was fine and told me to go to bed. They were going to stay up for awhile to talk.

I took out some sheets, blankets, and pillows and left them next to the sofa, telling them if they needed anything else not to worry about waking me. I walked into my bedroom and fell asleep right away; however, within a little while I woke up startled by a lot of hollering. I jumped out of bed and threw on my robe, hearing Mom and Dad yelling at each other. I looked out of my bedroom door. They didn't see me standing in the doorway.

They were both on their feet as if they were ready to start physically fighting. Mom stood as if she was going to take a swing at Dad. She yelled, "Joe! It was your fault! All your fault!" Dad yelled in Spanish, "No, Millie, it was yours! I would have stayed with you! You had no right to do what you did!"

I wondered what the neighbors were going to say. I knew everyone was awake in the apartment building because the walls were as thin as paper.

"Joe! I waited for you to straighten up, and you never did! You went out with other women? You expected me to sit at home and wait for you?"

"Sí, I did! And you should have!"

"No, no, no, Joe! I did for years, but I couldn't forever!"

Dad was standing there as if he wanted to slap Mom for events that occurred years ago. He then noticed me standing at the doorway. Mom looked my way also. They had both been drinking. She didn't drink very much in the past, although she liked going to clubs to dance.

Dad said, "Mijo, go back to bed." He glanced at Mom and said, "Sit down, Millie. Let's talk about this in a civilized way." He looked back at me and continued, "It's OK, Arthur. Go back to bed. We'll try not to make too much noise. But we have to talk about this because it has been many years that we have been carrying this around."

I told them I would return to bed and didn't say anything more. Returning to my bedroom and closing the door, I knew Dad would never strike Mom. No matter how angry he became at her when they were married, he never hit her.

I couldn't fall asleep and could hear them arguing. At times it became a little loud, but soon it quieted down again. In an hour-and-a-half, I fell asleep, periodically waking up when I heard their loud voices. I couldn't make out what they were saying most of the time, only words here and there. It reminded me of when I was a young boy, being in my bedroom, smothering my head under my covers and pillow while my father and mother argued about one thing or another.

I woke up at 4 a.m. to the sound of laughter. Mom and Dad were talking and laughing. I tried to listen to what they were saying but couldn't make out anything. I really wanted them to get along with each other.

At 7 a.m. I awoke and took a shower. As I stepped out of my bedroom, Mom and Dad was sitting on the couch, holding each other as Dad whispered, smoking his cigarette at the same time. They both were heavy smokers. Mom was resting her head on his chest, holding him as she listened to his words. It was a very good feeling for me to see them treating each other so tenderly.

"Good morning, Mijo," Dad greeted.

Mom lifted her head and smiled, "Good morning, Arthur."

"Good morning, Mom and Dad."

From that day forward, even though Mom and Dad had their own lives, they became best friends and remained friends until Dad's death.

View my Picture Album at www.EastSideDreams.com

ORDER FORM

Give a person a Gift.

No. of Copies:

_____**East Side Dreams by Art Rodriguez.** $13.95
(*Inspirational Story About Growing Up.*)

_____**The Monkey Box by Art Rodriguez.** (Romantic Family Story.) $12.95

_____**Forgotten Memories by Art Rodriguez.** (Sequel to East Side Dreams.) . $12.95

_____**Those Oldied but Goodies by Art Rodriguez.** $13.95
(*Sequel to East Side Dreams.*)

Shipping & handling, first copy $4.00 plus $1.00 for each additional copy.
Five books or more, Shipping & handling, NO CHARGE.
Make checks payable to **Dream House Press**. We are prompt about sending books out.

Check Number _____

Your Name _____

Street _____

City _____

State _____Zip _____

If you are paying with a credit card, you may fax or send to address below.

❏ Visa   ❏ MasterCard   ❏ American Express   ❏ Discover Card

Card Number _____

Expiration Date _____

Signature _____

Send to:
Dream House Press
2714 Ophelia Ct
San Jose, CA 95122

Phone: (408) 274-4574
Fax: (408) 274-0786
www.EastSideDreams.com